Here today, gone tomorrow. . . .

"These dead spots. I thought the spell we worked out prevented them," said Mendanbar.

"It should have," Telemain said, nodding. "And since the spell has worked perfectly well for over a year, it seems unlikely that the breakdown is due to an inherent flaw; nonetheless, I think the initial phase of our investigation should involve an examination and analysis of the primary linkages."

Cimorene blinked and looked at Mendanbar.

"He doesn't think there should be anything wrong with the spell, but he wants to check and make sure," Mendanbar translated. "In that case, we'll need the sword, won't we? I'll go get it." He snapped his fingers, and a small gold key materialized out of the air in front of him and dropped into his hand. An instant later, Mendanbar and the key vanished. A quiet huff of air rushed in to fill the space he had vacated.

A few moments later, air puffed outward as Mendanbar reappeared. His face was set in grim lines and his hands were empty. "It's gone," he said. "The lock on the chest has been melted to a puddle, the lid is up, and the sword is gone."

Calling
on
Dragons

READ ALL OF THE
ENCHANTED FOREST CHRONICLES
BY PATRICIA C. WREDE

Dealing with Dragons

Searching for Dragons

Calling on Dragons

Talking to Dragons

and

Book of Enchantments
featuring tales from the
Enchanted Forest

Calling on Dragons

THE ENCHANTED FOREST CHRONICLES
BOOK THREE

Patricia C. Wrede

MAGIC CARPET BOOKS
HARCOURT, INC.
Orlando Austin New York San Diego Toronto London

www.HarcourtBooks.com

First published 1993
First Magic Carpet Books edition 2003

Magic Carpet Books is a trademark of Harcourt, Inc., registered in the United States of America and/or other jurisdictions.

The Library of Congress has cataloged the hardcover edition as follows:
Wrede, Patricia C., 1953–
Calling on dragons/Patricia C. Wrede.
p. cm.—(The Enchanted Forest chronicles; bk. 3)
Sequel to: Dealing with dragons; Searching for dragons.
Sequel: Talking to dragons.
Summary: Queen Cimorene turns to her friends Morwen, Telemain, and Kazul for help when troublesome wizards make their way back into the Enchanted Forest and begin to soak up its magic.
[1. Fairy tales. 2. Magic—Fiction. 3. Wizards—Fiction. 4. Kings, queens, rulers, etc.—Fiction.] I. Title. II. Series: Wrede, Patricia C., 1953– Enchanted Forest chronicles; bk. 3.
PZ8.W92Cal 1993
[Fic]—dc20 92-35469
ISBN 0-15-200950-7
ISBN 0-15-204692-5 pb

Text set in Palatino
Designed by Dalia Hartman
Printed in the United States of America
C E G H F D

For my nieces and nephews,
with love and the hope
that they will grow up reading

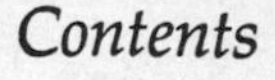

Contents

Calling
on
Dragons

1

In Which a Great Many Cats Express Opinions

Deep in the Enchanted Forest, in a neat gray house with a wide porch and a red roof, lived the witch Morwen and her nine cats. The cats were named Murgatroyd, Fiddlesticks, Miss Eliza Tudor, Scorn, Jasmine, Trouble, Jasper Darlington Higgins IV, Chaos, and Aunt Ophelia, and not one of them looked anything like a witch's cat. They were tabby, gray, white, tortoiseshell, ginger, seal brown, and every other cat color in the world except a proper and witchy black.

Morwen didn't look like a witch any more than her cats looked as if they should belong to one. For one thing, she was much too young—less than thirty—and she had neither wrinkles nor warts. In fact, if she hadn't been a witch people might have said she was quite pretty. Her hair was the same ginger color as Jasmine's fur, and she had hazel eyes and a delicate, pointed chin Because she was very short, she had to stand quite straight (instead of hunching over in correct witch fashion) if she wanted people to pay attention to her. And she was nearsighted, so she always had to wear glasses; hers had rectangular lenses. She refused even to put on the tall, pointed hats most witches wore, and she dressed in loose black robes because they were comfortable and practical, not because they were traditional.

All of this occasionally annoyed people who cared more about the propriety of her dress than the quality of her spells.

"You ought to turn him into a toad," Trouble said, looking up from washing his right front paw. Trouble was a large, lean gray tomcat with a crooked tail and a recently acquired ragged ear. He had never told Morwen exactly how he had damaged either the tail or the ear, but from the way he acted she assumed he had won a fight with something.

"Who should I turn into a toad?" Morwen asked, looking an unusually long way down. She was sitting sideways on her broomstick, floating comfortably next to the top of the front door, with a can of gold paint in one hand and a small paintbrush in the other. Above the door, in black letters partly edged in gold, ran the message "NONE OF THIS NONSENSE, PLEASE," which Morwen was engaged in repainting.

"That fellow who's making all the fuss about pointy hats and respect for tradition," Trouble replied. "The one you were grumbling about a minute ago—what's his name?"

"Arona Michaelear Grinogion Vamist," Morwen

recited, putting the final gold line along the bottom of the "L" in "PLEASE." "And it's a tempting thought. But someone worse would probably replace him."

"Turn them all into toads. I'll help."

"Toads?" purred a new voice. A small ginger cat slithered out the open window and arched her back, then stretched out along the window ledge, where she could watch the entire front yard without turning her head. "I'm tired of toads. Why don't you turn somebody into a mouse for a change?" The ginger cat ran her tongue around her lips.

"Good morning, Jasmine," Morwen said. "I'm not planning to turn anyone into anything, at the moment, but I'll keep it in mind."

"That means she won't do it," said Trouble. He looked at his right paw, decided it was clean enough for the time being, and began washing his left.

"Won't do what?" said Fiddlesticks, poking his brown head out of the front door. "Who's not doing it? Why shouldn't he—or is that she? And who says so?"

"Turn someone into a mouse; Morwen; I certainly don't see why not; and she does," Jasmine said in a bored tone, and pointedly turned her head away.

"Mice are nice." Fiddlesticks shouldered the door open another inch and trotted out onto the porch. "So are fish. I haven't had any fish in a long time." He paused underneath Morwen's broom and looked up expectantly.

"You had fish for dinner yesterday," Morwen said without looking down. "And you ate enough breakfast this morning to satisfy three ordinary cats, so don't try to pretend you're starving. It won't work."

"Someone's coming," Jasmine observed from the window.

Trouble stood up and ambled to the edge of the porch. "It's the Chairwitch of the Deadly Nightshade Gardening Club. Wasn't she just here last week?"

"It's Archaniz? Oh, bother," said Morwen, sticking her paintbrush into the can. "Has she got that idiot cat Grendel with her? I told her not to bring him anymore, but nine times out of ten she doesn't listen."

Fiddlesticks joined Trouble at the top of the porch steps. "I don't see him. I don't see anyone but her. I don't want to see her, either. She doesn't like me."

"That's because you talk too much," Trouble told him.

"I'm going inside," Fiddlesticks announced. "Then I won't have to see her. Maybe someone's dropped some fish on the floor," he added hopefully as he trotted into the house.

Morwen landed her broomstick and stood up, just as the Chairwitch reached the porch steps. The Chairwitch looked exactly as a witch ought: tall, with a crooked black hat, stringy black hair, sharp black eyes, a long, bony nose, and a wide, thin-lipped mouth. She hunched over as she walked, leaning on her broom as if it were a cane.

Morwen put the paint can on the window ledge next to Jasmine, set her broom against the wall, and said, "Good morning, Archaniz."

"Good morning, Morwen," Chairwitch Archaniz croaked. "What's this I hear about you growing lilacs in your garden?"

"Since I don't know what you've heard, I can't

answer you," Morwen replied. "Come in and have some cider."

Archaniz pounded the end of her broom against the porch floor, breaking some of the twigs and scattering bits of dust and bark in all directions. "Don't be provoking, Morwen. You're a witch. You're supposed to grow poison oak and snakeroot and wolfsbane, not lilacs. You'll get thrown out of the Deadly Nightshade Gardening Club if you aren't careful."

"Nonsense. Where in the rules does it say that I can't grow what I please in my own garden?"

"It doesn't," Archaniz admitted. "And I'll tell you right away that you aren't the only one who puts a few lilacs and daylilies in with the rampion and henbane. Why, I've got a perfectly ordinary patch of daisies in the corner myself."

"Daisies." Jasmine snorted softly. "She would."

"But I've been getting complaints," Archaniz continued, "and I have to do *something* about them."

"What sort of complaints?"

"That the Deadly Nightshade Gardening Club is too normal for witches," Archaniz said gloomily. "That all we grow are everyday plants like cabbages and apples—"

"Apples are a basic necessity for witches," Morwen said. "And everyday plants don't turn the people who eat them into donkeys. Who's complaining?"

"Some fellow with an impossible name—Arona Mc-something-or-other."

"Arona Michaelear Grinogion Vamist?"

The Chairwitch nodded. "That's the one. I've gotten six regular letters and two by Eagle Express in the past month. He says he's going to write a letter to the *Times* next."

"He would," Trouble muttered. "I *said* you should turn him into a toad."

"That idea sounds better all the time," Morwen told Trouble. Then she looked back at Archaniz, who of course had not understood a word Trouble had said. "Vamist isn't a witch," Morwen said. "He's an idiot. Why worry about what he says?"

"That's all very well, Morwen, but if he convinces people he's right, it'll ruin our image. And if people think we're not dangerous, they'll come around asking for love potions and penny curses whenever they like. We'll be so busy mixing up cures for gout that we won't have time for the things *we* want to do. Look what happened to the sorceresses!"

"I haven't seen many of them around lately."

Archaniz nodded. "They got a reputation for being kind and beneficent, and the next thing you knew everyone was begging them for help. Most of them moved to remote islands or deep forests, just to get away from the pestering. It's all very well for you, Morwen, living out here in the Enchanted Forest anyway, but I—"

A loud yowl interrupted the Chairwitch in mid-sentence. An instant later, four cats tore around the corner of the house. The one in front was a heavy, short-legged tomcat with yellow eyes and fur as black as night. Behind him came a fat, long-haired tabby tomcat and two females, one a large calico and the other a fluffy white cat with blue eyes. The black cat streaked out into the front yard, made a hairpin turn, and leapt for the porch, where he clawed his way up Archaniz's skirts to a perch on her shoulder.

The three pursuing cats jumped gracefully onto the porch railing and sat down, curling their tails around their feet, just as Fiddlesticks poked his head out of the front door.

"What's all the noise about? Who's shouting? Is it a fight? Who's winning? Can I join?" With every question, Fiddlesticks pushed a little farther, until he was entirely outside the house, staring up at Archaniz and the cat on her shoulder. "Who's *that?*"

"Mrow!" said the black cat in a complaining tone. "Yow wow mrrrum!"

"Oh, yeah?" said Trouble. "Well, *your* father wears *boots!*"

Morwen gave the black cat a speculative look. "One of these days, I am going to have to work up a spell that will let me understand other people's cats as well as my own," she said to Archaniz. "What was that about?"

"We caught him nosing around in back of the garden," the long-haired tabby growled.

"He had no business there," the white cat added primly. "He's not one of *us*, after all. So we thought we would drive him away."

"Stupid creature was babbling something about a rabbit," the calico cat said with a disdainful look at the black cat. "As if that was any excuse."

"Why didn't you call me?" Trouble demanded. "I never get to have any fun." Radiating hurt pride, he stalked to the far end of the porch and disappeared into a large clump of beebalm.

"You know, people have been trying to perfect a universal cat-translating spell for years," Archaniz said to Morwen in a dry tone. She glanced at the cats on the porch railing. "If you *do* come up with one, I'd like a copy for myself."

"Nosy old biddy," said the calico cat.

"On second thought, perhaps it would be better if I left things as they are," Morwen said.

"Being disagreeable, are they?" Archaniz said knowingly. "It's only to be expected. Who ever heard of a polite cat?"

The black cat hissed. "Grendel!" said Archaniz. "Behave yourself. It wasn't that bad, and besides, you can use the exercise."

"He certainly can," said the calico cat.

"What's all this racket?" rumbled a low, sleepy cat voice from under the porch. "Dash it, can't a fellow take a nap in peace?" A moment later, a long cream-and-silver cat oozed around the steps to blink at the growing assembly above him.

"That's another thing, Morwen," Archaniz said, scowling at the newcomer. "Cats and witches go together, I admit. And I know they're a big help with your spells, but one really ought to observe some reasonable limits."

"I do," said Morwen. All nine cats were useful, particularly when it came to working long, involved spells that required both concentration and power. Nine cats working together could channel a lot of magic. To explain all this would sound uncomfortably like bragging, however, so Morwen only added, "Anyway, I like cats."

"She is simply jealous because we're all smarter than *he* is," the white cat informed Morwen with a look at the black cat on Archaniz's shoulder.

"What, all of you?" Morwen said, raising an eyebrow.

"All of us," the white cat said firmly. "Even Fiddlesticks."

"I'm very smart," Fiddlesticks agreed. "I'm *lots* smarter than Fatso there. Don't you think I'm smart, Morwen?"

Grendel hissed and bunched together as if he were preparing to launch himself from Archaniz's shoulder. Hastily, Archaniz put up her free hand to hold him back. "Perhaps I had better leave now," she said. "We can finish our discussion some other—"

"There's a big garden show coming up in Lower Sandis," Morwen said thoughtfully. "Why doesn't the Deadly Nightshade Garden Club enter an exhibit? If we all work together, we should be able to put together something quite impressive."

Archaniz considered. "Monkshood and snakeroot and so on? In a large black tent."

"And if everyone sends one or two really exotic things—"

"Morwen, you're a genius! People will talk about it for years, and that Airy McAiling Grinny person won't have a leg to stand on."

"I don't think it will be that simple," Morwen cautioned. "But an exhibit will buy us time to find out why he's so interested in making witches do things *his* way. And stop him."

"Of course," the Chairwitch said happily. "Let's

see—Kanikak grows Midnight fire-flowers, and I have half a dozen Giant Weaselweeds. If I can talk Wully into letting us use her smokeblossoms . . ."

"I'll contribute two Black Diamond snake lilies and an invisible dusk-blooming chokevine," Morwen said. "I won't keep you any longer now; just let me know when you've got things arranged. Chaos, Miss Eliza, Scorn, wait for me inside, if you please."

The three cats sitting on the railing looked at each other. Then Chaos, the long-haired tabby, jumped down and sauntered past Fiddlesticks into the house. The white cat, Miss Eliza Tudor, followed, tail high, and Fiddlesticks fell in behind her, apparently without even thinking about what he was doing. Scorn sat where she was, staring stubbornly at Morwen.

"I'm not leaving while that idiot of hers is still here," Scorn said with a sidelong glance at Grendel and Archaniz. "There's no telling *what* he might get up to."

As this did not seem unreasonable, for a cat, Morwen let it pass. She walked Archaniz out into the yard, where there was plenty of room for a takeoff, and bade her a polite good-bye. As soon as the Chairwitch was out of sight above the trees, Morwen turned to go back inside. Jasper Darlington Higgins IV was sitting in front of the porch steps, watching her.

"Was that a good idea?" he said. "Invisible dusk-blooming chokevines aren't exactly easy to find, you know. Much less to grow. And you haven't got any, unless you've added them to the garden since early this morning."

"I'm well aware of that," Morwen said. "But I've been wanting some for a long time, to put along the fence by the back gate. Now I've got a good excuse to hunt them up."

"As long as you know what you're getting into," Jasper said. "Can I go back to sleep now, or is there going to be more noisy excitement?"

"Go to sleep," said Morwen. As she climbed the porch steps, she gave Scorn a pointed glare. Dignity dripping from every whisker, Scorn jumped down from the railing and walked into the house. Morwen shook her head, picked up her broomstick and her paint can, and followed.

2

In Which Morwen Encounters a Rabbit

Miss Eliza, Scorn, and Chaos were sitting in the kitchen, trying to look as if they were waiting for something interesting to happen and not as if they were doing as Morwen had told them. The only one who managed it was Scorn, who had jumped up onto the bench below the side window and begun washing her face. When Morwen entered, she looked up briefly and then returned to washing. In contrast, Chaos jumped guiltily and Miss Eliza Tudor looked away. There was no sign of Fiddlesticks.

"Archaniz has left, and Grendel has gone with her," Morwen said, setting the paint on the table. "Now, which of you three would like to begin?"

"Begin what?" Chaos asked warily.

Scorn stopped washing and snorted. "Don't be

dense. She wants to know about our chasing Grendel."

"We have already explained that," Miss Eliza said.

"Not to my satisfaction," Morwen said. "You know better than to pick a fight with another witch's cat. At least, I thought you did."

"It's our job to keep things out of the garden," Chaos said, looking up with his green eyes wide. "That's all we were doing."

Morwen sighed. "Well, at least I don't have to ask who started it. What happened, exactly?"

The cats exchanged looks. "We were out by the back fence, the three of us and Aunt Ophelia and Murgatroyd," Miss Eliza said. "Chaos was in the apple tree—"

"As usual," Scorn put in. "You'd think it belonged to him."

"—and he saw that witch swoop down over the hill behind the house. He said he saw her cat jump off the broomstick—"

"Probably looking for that blue catnip that grows on the far side," Scorn said. "Grendel's a little too fond of his nibbles, if you ask me."

"Nobody did," said Chaos.

Miss Eliza glared at the other two and lashed her tail. "*If* I may continue . . . ?"

"Nobody's stopping you," Scorn said, and to show her complete indifference she bent sideways and began washing her side.

"We were concerned," Miss Eliza went on. "It seemed unusual. A minute or two later, while we were discussing whether to do anything about it, that black cat came tearing over the hill and down toward the garden, shouting about some rabbit."

"Stupid excuse for a cat," Chaos muttered. "Running away from a *rabbit!* I ask you!"

Scorn merely snorted expressively.

Miss Eliza looked at them. "While I do not like all these interruptions, I must confess that I agree with you. It is *not* the kind of behavior one hopes for in a cat."

"So you couldn't resist tearing off after him." Morwen shook her head.

"He was heading for the garden," Chaos said, avoiding her eyes. "We were just doing our job."

"Murgatroyd and Aunt Ophelia stayed in back, in case the rabbit showed up," Miss Eliza Tudor offered.

"At least that much was well done," Morwen said. "I think—"

"Morwen? Morwen? Open the door and let me in. Morwen?" The new cat voice floated in through the back window.

With a faint frown, Morwen crossed to the far door and opened it. Immediately, Aunt Ophelia, a spiky tortoiseshell cat, shot through the opening and bounded onto a chair. "Thank goodness! I was afraid you weren't going to hear me."

"I thought you and Murgatroyd were watching for rabbits," Morwen said.

"We found one," said the tortoiseshell. "And I think you had better go look at it."

"I suppose it's got fangs," Scorn said, looking down her nose. "Or webbed feet."

"You needn't sneer at Ophelia," Miss Eliza said. "The last one I chased out of the sweetpeas had both."

"Where is this interesting rabbit?" Morwen asked.

"Heading for the back fence," Aunt Ophelia said

with poorly concealed relief. "Murgatroyd is in Chaos's apple tree, keeping an eye on it."

Morwen nodded and went out onto the back step. The garden seemed neat and peaceful, the square beds of vegetables on the left, the more exotic plants and herbs on the right. A shoulder-high row of new apple trees marched along the rear of the vegetable beds, just inside the picket fence. The first was just beginning to leaf out, the second was speckled with white blossoms, the third held a half-dozen marble-sized green fruit, and the fourth was beginning to drop its dark, rust-colored leaves as if in preparation for winter. At the far end of the garden stood a much older tree, heavily laden with apples that were just turning red. Below it, the back gate led out onto a grassy hill. An enormous lilac bush, nearly as tall as the apple tree, leaned over the fence on the right side of the gate.

There was no sign of Murgatroyd or of the interesting rabbit, so Morwen started toward the gate. Halfway there, she heard a thump and the top of the lilac thrashed violently.

"Murgatroyd?"

A loud hiss from the apple tree was followed by more thrashing in the lilac. "Get back, you, you—you *rabbit!*" snarled Murgatroyd's voice. "I warn you! Watch out, Morwen, it's in the lilac!"

"I suspected as much," Morwen said. "Exactly where—"

"Here," said a deep, mournful voice. "I'm stuck."

"If you break any of those branches, Morwen'll turn you into a lizard," Murgatroyd yelled from the apple.

"Lizards?" said Fiddlesticks from behind Morwen. "But I thought she was doing mice now."

"Quiet," Morwen said without looking back. "You in the lilac, hold still. Murgatroyd, stop making him nervous." She opened the gate and went slowly around the end of the lilac. "Now, then—good heavens."

Standing on the far side of the lilac was an enormous white rabbit. He was at least six feet tall, not counting the ears that drooped miserably down his back. Apart from his size, he did not seem unusual to Morwen: he had bright black eyes, a pink nose, and long whiskers. His front paw was caught in the branches of the lilac bush.

"I don't suppose you can do anything about this," the rabbit said gloomily. He tugged at his paw and the top of the lilac waved wildly to and fro.

From the apple tree, Murgatroyd hissed again. The rabbit cringed. "Stop that, both of you," Morwen commanded. "I think I can help if you'll hold still. What is your name, by the way?"

"Killer," said the rabbit in the same melancholy tone.

Morwen blinked, then shook her head. Rabbits had the oddest ideas about appropriate names. Perhaps it was because they had to come up with so many of them. She peered into the tangled heart of the lilac, then reached through the outer branches and tapped one of the fat trunks at the center. With a reluctant creak, the trunk bent slowly outward, freeing Killer's paw.

"My goodness," said the rabbit. He looked at his paw as if he were not quite sure it was properly attached, then shook it, then wiggled its toes. "My goodness gracious. Thank you very much, ma'am."

"Morwen. And I would still like that explanation."

A low, warning growl of agreement came out of the apple tree, and a moment later Murgatroyd scrambled down through the apple's branches to the fence rail.

Killer gave the cat a nervous look and began backing away. "It isn't a very interesting story. I'm sure you all have better things to do."

"All?" Morwen glanced back over her shoulder. Fiddlesticks, Miss Eliza, Aunt Ophelia, Jasmine, Trouble, Chaos, and Scorn were lined up in a long row at the bottom of the garden, staring at the rabbit. They made an intimidating picture. When Morwen looked at Killer again, he had retreated another couple of feet. Morwen glared.

"I, ah, was just going," said the rabbit. "You see, I'm late."

"For what?" Morwen demanded.

"Something important, I'm sure. Not that it matters. I'm always late, you see. It runs in the family; my brother even got himself a big gold pocket watch, and he still can't get anywhere on time."

"In that case, it won't matter if you're a little later. How did you happen to get caught in my lilac bush?"

The rabbit sighed. "I wanted something to eat, and this thing—you say it's a lilac?—looked large enough for a meal. It takes a lot to fill me up, now that I'm so big. Only I couldn't reach the bit I wanted, and when I tried, the branches twisted around and I got stuck, and then *he* snarled at me—" Killer broke off, cringing, as Murgatroyd demonstrated the snarl for Morwen's benefit.

Morwen frowned at the rabbit. "How long have you been six feet tall?"

"Seven feet, eleven inches," corrected Killer, "counting the ears. Since this morning. And it's no fun, believe me. I'm hungry all the time, and I don't fit in my hole, and I can't hide under bushes the way I used to."

"And how did you happen to grow so large so quickly?"

"I don't know." Killer sighed again and his ears lifted and dropped expressively. "I was just nibbling at my clover patch when all of a sudden everything started shrinking. The next thing I knew, I was nearly eight feet tall—counting the ears—and there wasn't enough clover for a snack, much less breakfast. It didn't even taste right," he finished sadly.

"Before or after you started growing?"

The rabbit's ears stiffened as he frowned in concentration. "The taste? Before. Definitely before. The leaves were a little sour and the stems didn't crunch right."

It sounded as if some enchanted seeds had gotten mixed in with the clover, and Killer had eaten the sprouts. If Morwen was lucky, he wouldn't have eaten all of them. A plant that increased one's size would be a valuable addition to the garden, even if it only worked on rabbits. "I'd like to see this clover patch."

"Well . . ." Killer hesitated. "Do you have to bring *them?* I don't like cats."

"I don't think I'll need everyone," Morwen said.

"Aunt Ophelia, Trouble, and Miss Eliza will be quite enough."

"Why can't I come?" Fiddlesticks trotted up to the gate and inspected the rabbit through the slits. "I didn't get to chase Fatso, and I didn't get to chase the rabbit. My, he's big. And I didn't get any fish."

"You talk too much, that's why," Trouble told him.

"Perhaps you should go tell Jasper what's happened," Miss Eliza put in.

"Right," said Fiddlesticks. "Maybe he's caught a mouse while we've been out here talking to rabbits. Maybe he'll share!" And he bounded off.

"Optimist," said Scorn, looking after him.

"If we are going to look at *vegetables*," said Aunt Ophelia in tones that conveyed her poor opinion of the entire undertaking, "perhaps we should get it over with."

"Are you done for now, Morwen?" Jasmine asked. "Because if you are, I'm going back to the window before someone else grabs it."

"Go ahead," Morwen told her. Immediately, Jasmine and Scorn took off at a dead run for the house. Morwen turned to the rabbit. "Now, about this clover patch . . ."

Killer dropped to all fours, which brought his head nearly level with Morwen's. He sniffed the air twice and cocked an ear to the right. "That way." He started off, and Morwen and the three chosen cats followed.

After ten minutes, Morwen was wishing she had brought her broomstick. Killer set an extremely uneven pace, taking two or three long hops that would nearly carry him out of sight and then pausing to sniff the air and twitch his whiskers nervously. It would have been much easier to follow him by air, Morwen thought, but she did not say anything because it would only encourage the cats to complain. Trouble, in particular, was extremely put out at having to let a rabbit lead. To make up for it, he pretended to stalk Killer, slinking around trees like a gray shadow and muttering under his breath. Aunt Ophelia and Miss Eliza contented themselves with making malicious remarks. Fortunately, Killer was usually too far ahead to hear any of them.

When they finally reached the clover patch, Mor[illegible]en was nearly as cross as her cats. Killer did not seem [illegible] notice. He sat back on his haunches, waved proudly, [illegible]nd said, "Here we are!"

"This is it?" Trouble said, staring at an irregular mat of small green plants. It was no more than four feet across, and a third of the plants had been nipped neatly off, leaving only short, bare stems. "That's *all?*"

"It's much larger when I'm my normal size," Killer said in an apologetic tone. "And it's got much better flavor than the one by the little pond or the one by the currant bush. At least, it used to."

Morwen suppressed a sigh of irritation. As long as she'd come this far, she'd better have a look at the thing, even if it didn't seem particularly promising. Pushing her glasses firmly into their proper position—they had slid down her nose a little on the walk—she knelt beside the clover patch.

At first glance, nothing looked out of the ordinary. Trouble came up beside her and sniffed at the plants. "Don't nibble on any of them," Morwen said.

"I'm not *stupid*," said Trouble.

"No, but you've done things like that before," Aunt Ophelia put in. "Don't interrupt Morwen while she's working."

Trouble licked his front paw twice, displaying his unconcern to the world at large, then pounced on an imaginary mouse in the middle of the clover patch.

"Morwen, there's something rather odd over here," Miss Eliza said. She was crouched at the opposite edge of the clover patch, and her tail was lashing back and forth in a way that belied her casual tone. "When you have a moment, you may wish to look at it closely."

"I'll take a moment now," Morwen said, rising. "What is it?"

"These." Miss Eliza sat back and waved a paw at the moss in front of her. A six-inch strip next to the clover patch was peppered with small brown spots, as if someone had pushed the end of a pencil into it several times.

"You're quite right," Morwen said. "This is odd. Killer, do you remember which part of this patch you were nibbling on when you started to grow?"

"Not really. Does it matter?"

"It might. Trouble, would you please look around and see whether you can find any more of these spots?"

"Oh, all right," said Trouble, but his yellow eyes gleamed with pleasure as he circled the clover patch.

"What are they?" Aunt Ophelia asked, joining Miss Eliza at Morwen's side. "Besides odd."

"I don't know. They *look* like a small version of—"

"Morwen!" Trouble yelled from the foot of a nearby tree. "Here's a big one!"

With a sinking feeling, Morwen crossed to Trouble's side, followed by the other cats. In the moss at the foot of the tree, just where someone might have set the end of a staff to lean against the trunk, was a dead brown circle about two inches across.

"A wizard!" Morwen said. "I was afraid of this."

3

In Which Morwen Makes a Discovery and Some Calls

There was an instant of silence, and then all of the animals tried to talk at once.

"One at a time, please," Morwen said. "Or I won't understand a thing any of you are trying to say. Killer first."

"The *rabbit?*" Trouble curled his lip back, showing his fangs in an expression that wasn't quite a snarl. "Why *him?*"

"Courtesy to a guest," Morwen replied. "Killer?"

"It's just a hole in the moss," said the rabbit. "It doesn't look like a wizard to me."

"Of course *that*'s not a wizard," Aunt Ophelia said. "*That* is what a wizard's staff does when it touches a part of the Enchanted Forest. I thought everyone knew that."

"He obviously hasn't been paying attention to the news for at least a year," Miss Eliza said. "Possibly longer." She switched her tail. "Are you even aware that the King of the Enchanted Forest has been married for nearly fourteen months?"

"Stop badgering," Morwen said to the cats. "And remember that you are in something of a privileged position when it comes to news from the castle." She turned to Killer. "Queen Cimorene has been a friend of mine since before the wedding, and we still keep in touch."

"You knew about the wizards' staffs long before then," Miss Eliza objected.

"Knew what about wizards' staffs?" Killer's ears swiveled from the cats to Morwen. "That they make holes in the forest?"

"Exactly," Morwen said. "Wizards' staffs absorb magic from anything that happens to be around. Unfortunately, in the Enchanted Forest *everything* is magical, one way or another, and when a staff soaks up enough magic it kills part of the forest."

"And this certainly looks like the kind of thing that happens when a wizard sets down the end of his staff," Miss Eliza said. "Careless creatures."

"Well, if this bit is from a wizard's staff, what made all those tiny dots back by that clover patch?" Aunt Ophelia said. "Miniature wizards?"

"Quite possibly," Morwen replied. "If a wizard worked a size-changing spell in this area and let a little spill over into the clover patch, it would explain Killer's unusual growth very nicely."

Miss Eliza's nose twitched as if she smelled something unpleasant. "I *said* they were careless."

"Yes, but look, Morwen, this can't be wizards," Trouble said. "The King chased all of them out of the forest before he got married."

"One of them seems to have come back," Morwen said, looking pointedly at the bare spot. "And I think we had better notify the King immediately."

"Couldn't you just, uh, plant something new in the hole and forget about it?" asked Killer nervously. "I mean, the King must have more important things to do than worry about my clover patch."

All three of the cats swiveled their heads and stared at him with disapproval.

The rabbit's ears wilted under their combined gaze. "It was just a thought."

"On the contrary," said Miss Eliza.

Aunt Ophelia shrugged. "What do you expect from a rabbit?"

"It's the wizards that are important, not your clover," said Trouble. "If there *are* wizards."

"Nothing else I know of does *that*." Morwen pointed at the hole.

"Just because you don't know of it doesn't mean there isn't something," Trouble retorted.

"Mmhmph. I suppose you're right." Morwen considered for a moment. She couldn't tell whether the holes had been made by a wizard's staff or not, but she knew at least three people who could. The first two were the King of the Enchanted Forest and his Queen, Cimorene. The third . . . "I'd better give Telemain a call, then, as well as Mendanbar and Cimorene. If we're lucky, he'll think it's a fascinating challenge."

"And if we're not, he'll prose on about it for hours," Trouble muttered.

"Who's Tele-whatsis?" asked Killer.

"An old friend and magical theoretician," Morwen said. "He's interested in wizards."

"Among other things." Trouble poked his nose into the brown spot, then pulled it back very quickly and sneezed. "Can we go now?"

Morwen started back toward the clover patch. "As soon as I take a sample of Killer's clover."

"I guess I'll be going, then," Killer said, backing away as he spoke. "Nice meeting you and all that."

"Don't be silly," Morwen said over her shoulder. "You're coming with us. I want you to tell your story to Telemain and the King. And how else are you going to get a decent meal?"

The rabbit didn't answer, and Morwen stopped paying attention to him. Kneeling next to the clover patch once more, she reached into the loose left sleeve of her robe, which she used as a sort of enchanted backpack. The spell on her sleeves allowed her to carry around all kinds of useful things, but it required a certain amount of concentration to retrieve them. And, of course, she had to remember what she had put into the sleeve in the first place.

"Sample jars," she muttered to herself. "Small sample jars with the lids that clamp down—ah!" With a smile of satisfaction, she pulled a glass jar the size of her fist out of the sleeve. The glass had a faint purple tint, and the lid was a glass bubble that was attached to the jar with a complicated-looking wire clamp. Morwen flicked the wire with her thumb, and the lid popped up. She could hear Killer and the cats arguing in the background, but she refused to listen. Reaching into her sleeve once more, she took out a small pair of herb snips and began cutting clover.

By the time the jar was half-full, the argument had stopped and the animals had joined her. Half a jar was enough, for now, Morwen decided. She clamped the lid down and put the jar and snips back into her sleeve, then rose, dusting bits of clover off her hands.

"Are you all ready to go now?" she asked.

"Yes," said Miss Eliza.

"No," said Killer. Trouble glared at him. "I mean, yes. I suppose so. Oh, I don't *like* cats!"

"That's what comes of being a rabbit," Aunt Ophelia said. "Size makes no difference whatsoever."

"Come along, then," Morwen said, and started briskly off in the direction of the house. The sooner she got home and relayed her news to the King, the better.

When they arrived home, the other cats were lined up in the garden, waiting for them. Chaos was loudly surprised to see that the rabbit was still tagging along, and Fiddlesticks demanded explanations and fish in the same breath, while Jasmine pretended to find the whole affair boring beyond expression.

"You'll just have to wait a bit longer," Morwen said over the racket. "I've work to do. In the meantime, try to remember that Killer is a guest."

"Killer?" said Fiddlesticks. "Who's Killer?"

"The rabbit, you idiot," Trouble told him as Morwen went into the house.

The closing door cut off whatever else Trouble might have had to say. Morwen shook her head but did not go back outside. As long as the cats left Killer alone and didn't damage each other too much, it was better to let them settle matters among themselves. Frowning in concentration, Morwen reached into her sleeve and pulled out the sample jar of clover. She set it on the kitchen table, then turned around and went out through the door by which she had just entered.

The door now led into her study. Making that door—and the various rooms it led to—had taken Morwen a great deal of time and effort, considerably more than her sleeves, but it had been worth every minute. She had added a library, a study, several bedrooms for visitors, a magic workshop, and a large storage area since she moved in, and all without using up any of the garden. And there was still space for three or four more rooms, if she needed them, before she'd have to add a second magic door.

Frowning slightly, Morwen skirted the cluttered desk and stopped in front of an oval mirror in the corner. The silvered glass was the size of a serving platter, and it was surrounded by a gilt frame three inches wide. The effect was a little too elaborate for Morwen's taste, but when someone makes one a present of a state-of-the-art magic mirror, one doesn't turn it down simply because it doesn't fit in with one's decor. *I suppose I'll get used to it eventually,* she thought. *After all, I only got around to hanging it this morning.*

"All right, let's see if this thing works as well as he said it would," she muttered. Taking a deep breath, she said clearly,

"Mirror, mirror, on the wall,
I would like to make a call."

Immediately, the mirror turned milky white and a pleasant voice from somewhere inside the glass said, "What party are you calling, please?"

"The King of the Enchanted Forest," Morwen answered, impressed in spite of herself. Telemain had been right; this was an enormous improvement over the mirrors Morwen had used in the past. And on top of that, it was polite.

"One moment, please," said the mirror.

Almost before it finished speaking, the glass cleared. Morwen blinked, startled. The face looking out at her was dark brown, with bulging eyes and a wide mouth full of crooked teeth. "This is the castle of the King of the Enchanted Forest, you lucky person," said the face with a leer. "Nobody else is here to answer the mirror, so you're gonna have to leave a message with—oh, it's you."

By this time, Morwen had recognized the bad-tempered wooden gargoyle that occupied the upper corner of King Mendanbar's study. "Good morning, gargoyle. Do Mendanbar and Cimorene know how you answer their mirror?"

The gargoyle snorted. "It was her idea. She thought it might cut down on the stupid questions people ask."

"I might have guessed. Where are they? I've got some news they should hear right away."

"They've gone to the beach with Kazul," the gargoyle said in tones of disgust. "Work's piling up, but do they care? No! Do they even ask if it's a good idea? No! They just pack a bag of towels and take off. Poof!"

"I see. In that case—"

"He humors her too much," the gargoyle went on

confidentially. "She's healthy as a horse, but you wouldn't know it, the way he fusses over her. And I'm going to have to put up with it for another six or seven months, at least! What he'll be like when the baby actually arrives—well, all I can say is that I'm going to have a full-time job trying to see that the kid isn't spoiled rotten."

"I expect Cimorene will help," Morwen said. "How soon will they be back?"

"How should I know? I'm not a secretary."

"Well, as soon as they arrive—*either* of them—tell them that I've reason to think that there's a wizard running around in the forest."

The gargoyle's eyes widened, making him look even uglier than before. "A wizard? Hoo boy!"

"I'm going to call Telemain next," Morwen went on. "If we're not here when they call back, tell them to come on out anyway. The cats can show them how to find us."

"I bet," the gargoyle muttered. "Anything else? 'Cause if there isn't, I'm going back to sleep."

"That's all," Morwen said, and the mirror clouded over. As soon as it cleared, she repeated the rhyme and snapped, "Telemain," in response to the mirror's polite question.

This time it took much longer for the glass to clear. When it did, Telemain's face scowled out of the mirror. His ferocious expression lightened only fractionally when he saw who was calling.

"Oh, hello, Morwen! Will this take long? I've just set up an exceedingly sensitive spell to test the stability quotient of—"

"It's wizards," Morwen interrupted. "Well, one of

them, at the very least, though in my experience whenever one turns up a half-dozen more are sure to follow. They're worse than cockroaches."

"You're in a poor humor this morning." Telemain ran a hand across his neat black beard, a sure sign that he was interested but didn't want to show it. "What about this wizard?"

"He appears to have been poking around near my home," Morwen said. "Or so I conclude from the splotches his staff left in the moss."

Telemain shook his head. "That is quite impossible. The warding enchantment that Mendanbar and I worked out keeps wizards from absorbing, manipulating, utilizing, or controlling any portion of the magical basis on which the Enchanted Forest is founded. So even if a wizard were unwise enough to enter the forest, his staff could not possibly leave, er, 'splotches in the moss.' "

"I know it's *supposed* to work that way," Morwen said. "But the splotches are there. So is a six-foot rabbit—this wizard is careless as well as nosy and impossible. If you don't believe me, come and look at them yourself."

"I believe I shall," Telemain said. "It'll only take me a few minutes to set up the transportation spell, and firsthand observation is always superior to reports from even the most reliable of witnesses. Now, let me see; I had better bring the microdynometer, and some detection instruments, and—"

He turned away, muttering to himself, and the mirror blanked abruptly. Morwen rolled her eyes.

"He's in rare form today," said Aunt Ophelia from behind her. "What was that about 'reliable witnesses'?"

Turning, Morwen saw the tortoiseshell cat standing just inside the open study door. "Since it came from Telemain, I'd have to say it was a compliment."

"Someone should take him in hand before he talks himself into a real mess."

"He can take care of himself," Morwen said. "If he couldn't, someone would have murdered him years ago. I've been tempted a time or two myself." Out of habit, she glanced around the study to see if there was anything she needed. Then she walked out to the kitchen and picked up the can of paint she'd abandoned there after Archaniz's visit. With a little luck, she could finish touching up the sign over the door before any of her visitors arrived.

4

In Which Morwen and Telemain Argue and Killer Discovers the Perils of Mixing Cosmetics and Magic

By the time Telemain appeared in the front yard, Morwen had finished the sign and was cleaning her brush. He did a tidy transportation spell, Morwen had to admit, even if her own taste ran more to flying. The passage hadn't even ruffled his dark hair. He'd clearly come prepared: The many pockets of his open knee-length black vest were bulging, and so were the pouches that hung from his wide black belt. Seven magic rings glittered on his fingers, three on his left hand, four on his right. His bright blue eyes were alight with anticipation.

"Well, it's about time," Aunt Ophelia said acidly as he walked up the porch steps.

"Hello to you, too," Telemain said, nodding far more politely than he would have if he'd understood her comment. "There you are, Morwen! Where are these hypothetical wizards of yours?"

"I bet he doesn't even know which one of us you are," Scorn said from the porch rail. "Hypothetical wizards, indeed!"

"What's that?" Fiddlesticks shouted from inside the house.

On the window ledge, Jasmine yawned, curling up her tongue and stretching her head back. Then she called back, "Telemain's here."

"Who's here?" Fiddlesticks poked his head around the edge of the door. "Telemain! Chaos, Murgatroyd, Trouble, Telemain's here!"

"Chaos and Trouble are watching that *rabbit*," said Miss Eliza, in a tone that indicated clearly that she would have liked very much to call it something else but was far too polite to actually do so.

"If I knew where the wizards were, I wouldn't need your help," Morwen said to Telemain. "The dead spots in the moss are about twenty minutes' walk from my back garden, if the forest hasn't moved them."

"Twenty minutes! Morwen, I don't have time—"

"I'd have told you to transport straight there, but I don't think you've been to the place before, and there's no sense in taking chances. Besides, it'll only take two minutes by broomstick, even riding double and with an extra load."

Telemain shook his head. "No. No. Absolutely not. I have no intention of riding on that uncomfortable contraption of yours ever again. Once was quite enough."

"Wimp," said Scorn.

"You only think broomsticks are uncomfortable because you insist on riding astride," Morwen said to Telemain. "If you'd sit sidesaddle, the way you're supposed to—"

"No!"

"Well, if you really want to hand-carry a bucket of soapy water mixed with a little lemon juice on a twenty-minute walk—"

"What? Morwen, you didn't say anything about buckets."

"Water?" Fiddlesticks sat up very straight, his nose twitching. "Buckets of water? With *soap?* Maybe I won't come with you this time, either, Morwen."

"I thought the buckets were obvious," Morwen told Telemain. "If there are wizards around, I want to be able to get rid of them in a hurry." And the only way to do that, so far as anyone knew, was to dump a bucket of soapy water mixed with a little lemon juice over the top of them. For some reason, this made them melt into a gooey puddle, and it usually took several days for them to put themselves together again. Cim orene had discovered the method by accident, back when she was living with the dragon Kazul.

"Soapy water," Telemain muttered. "Buckets. I still say it's terribly inelegant."

"If you'd finish working out a spell to do the same thing, the buckets wouldn't be necessary," Morwen pointed out.

Telemain flushed. "I've designed a prototype, but it requires the immediate accessibility of a target. It has therefore been impossible for me to run the necessary tests to ascertain its effectiveness."

"What?" said Fiddlesticks.

"He's invented a spell for melting wizards, but he

can't tell whether it works because there aren't any wizards around to try it on," Miss Eliza said.

"Oh. Why couldn't he just say that?"

"Because that's how he is," said Aunt Ophelia.

"We still need the buckets," Morwen said to Telemain. "I haven't the slightest objection to your testing your new wizard-melting spell on any wizards we run across, but I want to bring something that I *know* works, in case your spell needs some adjusting."

"Reasonable." Telemain rubbed his chin thoughtfully. "But I still categorically refuse to travel on that broomstick of yours."

"Morwen?" Even muffled by the front door, Trouble's tone was clearly far too casual, and when he strolled out onto the porch Morwen felt a strong twinge of misgiving. Every whisker dripped the kind of deliberate unconcern that usually meant he'd been living up to his name.

"Excuse me a moment, Telemain," Morwen said. "What is it, Trouble?"

"You know that rabbit you wanted us to watch?"

Morwen's misgivings deepened. "Yes?"

"Well, he's kind of upset," Trouble said. "Murgatroyd thought I'd better come tell you."

If Murgatroyd thought Morwen should be told about it, it was probably serious. Not urgent, though, or he'd have come himself, at a dead run. And he didn't expect Morwen to be happy about it, or he wouldn't have sent Trouble. Morwen sighed. "What is Killer upset about?"

"Oh, things. I wouldn't have bothered you if Murgatroyd hadn't insisted."

"Such a fuss about a *rabbit.*" Aunt Ophelia sniffed.

Trouble studied the porch roof, as if he were hoping to spot a fly. "Not exactly."

"I see." Morwen turned to Telemain. "I appear to be needed in the garden. You're welcome to come along."

"Certainly."

All of the cats followed them, except Jasmine, who had fallen asleep on the window ledge, and Jasper, who was presumably still napping under the porch. When they reached the garden, they found the grass inside the gate trampled flat and a six-foot donkey with a blotchy brown-and-white coat standing next to the vegetable patch. The donkey wore a mournful expression, and half a cabbage leaf was stuck to the side of his muzzle. The green cabbage directly in front of him was missing a large chunk from its left side.

"Hello, Killer," Morwen said to the donkey.

"I thought Killer was a rabbit," Telemain said, frowning in mild puzzlement.

"He was, until he started eating my cabbage." Morwen eyed the donkey reprovingly.

"He *ate* a *cabbage?*" Fiddlesticks said, horrified. "Why would he do *that?*"

"I was hungry," said the donkey. His tail switched and he jumped, startled.

"Hmph," said Aunt Ophelia. "Just what I'd expect from a rabbit."

"Yes, you'd think anyone would have more sense than to nibble on plants in a witch's garden," Miss Eliza said.

"I thought the gray cat said it was all right. And

it tasted very nice. Almost spicy. And the crunch—" The donkey stopped as all the cats glared, and his ears drooped. "I must have misunderstood."

Morwen glanced around. Trouble was nowhere in sight. "I don't think you misunderstood him at all." She looked sternly at Chaos and Murgatroyd. "Why didn't you stop him?"

"You've got plenty of donkey-cabbages," Chaos said. "And donkeys are nearly as stupid as rabbits, so it's not as if Killer lost anything by it."

"I think it's a definite improvement," Murgatroyd said, nodding.

"A six-foot donkey doesn't look nearly as silly as a six-foot rabbit," Aunt Ophelia put in.

"Seven feet, eleven inches, counting the ears," said the donkey, twitching them. "I always know how big I am."

"That is not the point," Morwen told the cats. "You were left here to prevent any untoward happenings. This is an extremely untoward happening. I am seriously displeased."

"And you know what that means," Scorn said. "No fish in the food bowl tonight."

"No fish?" Fiddlesticks looked up at Morwen with large, distressed eyes. "Not even for me?"

"I'm sorry about this, Killer," Morwen said. "Those cabbages aren't supposed to work on rabbits." She paused, considering. The red cabbages on the other side of the row were an antidote, but she wasn't sure she wanted to mention that. It was entirely possible that they wouldn't work, or that Killer would end up turning into a twelve-foot-tall rabbit or something even more inconvenient.

"Can't you do anything?" the donkey said. "It's not that I mind being a donkey, exactly, but I don't like what it did to my coat."

"He *is* awfully blotchy," Scorn said.

"Interesting," Telemain murmured. "You say these plants aren't supposed to work on rabbits, Morwen? And this rabbit was already under the influence of a magnifying enchantment. So the layered interaction of the two magical energies produces a synergistic effect . . ."

Killer looked at Telemain, and his ears twitched forward. "Is that why my coat is all funny?"

"Highly unlikely," Telemain said. "The two spells seem to affect primarily the parameters of form and stature, rather than coloration."

Morwen stared at the donkey. Suddenly her eyes narrowed. "Killer, do you dye your fur?"

"I, um—well, actually . . ."

"I thought so. That's what your problem is. Spells are hard on cosmetic changes. The dye job lasted through one spell, but now that you've been enchanted twice it's wearing off."

"Oh *no*," said Killer. "You mean if you turn me back into a rabbit, I'll look even *worse?*"

"Probably," Morwen said. "And you won't be able to redye it until the residue of the spell wears off. That usually takes about six weeks."

"How do you know all this?" Telemain asked her.

Morwen gave him a look. "Why do you think witches never color their hair?"

"This is terrible." Killer's ears waggled in distress, and several of the cats snickered. "I won't be able to hold up my head. This is *awful*. Can't you do anything?"

"Not right now," Morwen said. "We have some wizard hunting to do. And if you're willing to help, you may have solved a little problem for us."

"I don't mind being helpful," said Killer. "What problem?"

Morwen turned to Telemain. "You can ride *him* instead of the broomstick. He knows how to find the clover patch, and at that size he ought to move fairly quickly. I'll take the broomstick and a bucket and meet you there. And you can study the interaction of the size- and shape-changing spells on the way."

Less than ten minutes later, Morwen, Telemain, and Killer met at the half-eaten patch of clover. As Morwen landed her broomstick—with some care, so as not to spill the bucket she had hung on the front end—Scorn and Fiddlesticks slid out of the bushes and sat down at the foot of the nearest tree. The two cats wore identical smug expressions.

"What are you doing here?" Morwen said.

"We all discussed it and decided you might need help," Scorn replied. "Aunt Ophelia and Miss Eliza came last time, Trouble and Murgatroyd and Chaos are in disgrace because of the cabbages, and Jasmine didn't want to be bothered. So it came down to the three of us."

"*Three* of you?"

"Jasper's around somewhere."

"I came because I'm very brave," Fiddlesticks announced. He rose and sauntered over to the clover patch. "Don't you think I'm brave, Morwen? What's all this prickly stuff?" He sniffed at the bare stalks on the eaten portion of the patch.

"That's Killer's clover patch," Morwen said. "Don't eat any of it."

"*Eat* it?" Fiddlesticks looked up, green-gold eyes wide. "Why would I eat it? It's some kind of *plant*."

"We know," Scorn said. "Shut up."

Telemain slid down from Killer's back, stepped quickly to one side, and shook himself as if to check that everything still worked. Then he walked over to Morwen. With a glance over one shoulder to make sure Killer was out of hearing distance, he said in a low voice, "Morwen, this is absolutely the last time I agree to one of your . . . your ideas. That beast has a gait that would rattle the teeth out of a troll."

"It's not my fault," Killer said. "I'm supposed to be a rabbit."

Telemain looked startled, then chagrined.

"You forgot how long his ears are," Morwen said. "Never mind. The tracks I told you about are over here."

She led the way to the cluster of brown pencil-sized holes at the far side of the clover patch. When he saw them, Telemain immediately lost interest in the rest of his surroundings.

"Fascinating," he murmured. He pulled something that looked like a bright metal tube in a wire cage from one of his pockets and began twisting and pulling and unfolding. In less than two minutes, he held a small telescope attached to three long, spidery legs. He jabbed the legs into the moss and peered through the end of the telescope. "Absolutely fascinating. The residual energy displays the characteristic spiral, but its concentration—"

"Tell me about it when you decide what it is," Morwen said. She was in no mood for one of Telemain's long digressions into magical theory, even if she was one of the few people who actually understood most of what he said. Besides, listening only encouraged him.

Telemain peered through his telescope again, then pulled out several other peculiar instruments and poked at the holes. Finally he looked up. "Where's the other one?"

"Other one?" Morwen said. Even when he was being simple, Telemain didn't seem to be able to make himself clear.

"The full-sized, er, splotch. I believe you said there was one?"

"Trouble found it." Leaving Killer to nibble disconsolately at the moss and the cats to wander as they pleased, Morwen led Telemain to the two-inch circle of brown moss. "There."

"This is really amazing. Look here, Morwen, along the perimeter. There's no regeneration occurring at all. And—"

"Yes, of course," Morwen interrupted. "But all I want to know is, is it wizards?"

"Oh, certainly. That's what I was saying," Telemain replied with maddening innocence. "And it looks as if they've figured out how to evade the enchantment the King and I worked out. You were quite right to call me."

"Quite right?" Scorn said with considerable indignation. "That self-centered, conceited idiot! Of course you were quite right. Magicians, bah!" Tail stiff with disapproval, she stalked off.

"Exactly," said Morwen. "Now, what was the bit about that enchantment of yours?"

"Of mine and the King's." Telemain was a stickler for accuracy, even when it meant sharing the credit for a major magical achievement. He pointed at the brown spot in front of him, then waved back toward the clover patch. "None of these should be here."

"Well, obviously. Wizards aren't supposed to come into the Enchanted Forest any—" Morwen stopped short. "That isn't what you meant. Very well. Explain what you *did* mean, and none of your jargon. I've too much on my mind already without trying to unravel your sentences."

Telemain looked hurt. "I'm only trying to be precise."

"Right now I'll be quite content with fast and sloppy. Now, why shouldn't there be any dead patches in the moss?"

"Because the spell Mendanbar and I worked out should—should repair them as soon as they're made," Telemain said carefully. "As long as the spell is working, the absorptive properties of the wizard's staff should be balanced immediately by the recirculation of—"

"Telemain!"

"I'm trying," Telemain said in a plaintive tone. "There just isn't any other way to say it."

"No?" Morwen thought for a minute. "How about

this: When a wizard's staff sucks up magic from the forest, your spell sucks it back. And it works so fast that the moss shouldn't die this way."

"Or it should regenerate," Telemain said, nodding. "This has obviously not done either."

"Can you tell how they did it?"

"Not without an examination of the primary linkages." Telemain frowned down at the dead moss. "If something has damaged one of them, it might account—"

A loud cat squall erupted from behind a nearby bush, followed by a high shriek. Morwen started forward, but before she had taken two steps, Fiddlesticks came trotting around the left side of the bush. He held his head very high, and his tail was a long brown exclamation mark. Dangling from his mouth by a bunched-up wad of blue-and-brown wizard's robes was a man about six inches tall.

5

In Which the Plot Thickens

Fiddlesticks halted just in front of Morwen's feet. The man he was carrying kicked, then tried to punch backward and overhead at the cat's nose. Fortunately, he missed. Fiddlesticks growled and shook his head, and the man shrieked as he swung back and forth.

"How interesting," Telemain said. "Morwen, your cat appears to have captured a miniature wizard."

"So I see," Morwen said. "What did you do with his staff?"

"Mmmph hmmmph uff," said Fiddlesticks, and jabbed his tail back toward the bush.

"Good. Don't let him anywhere near it." Morwen turned and started for the clover patch.

"Where are you going?" Telemain said.

"To get the bucket," Morwen called over her shoulder. There was another high-pitched shriek from the wizard and a jumbled protest from Telemain, both of which she ignored. Having collected her bucket, she returned to find the wizard on his feet with Fiddlesticks standing guard. Telemain sat cross-legged in front of them, holding something that looked like a silver watch with an orange dial and four hands. He kept looking from the watch to the wizard and back.

"Has he told you what they're up to yet?" Morwen said, setting the bucket down a little to one side, where it would be handy but out of the immediate way.

Telemain looked up, frowning. "I haven't asked. Do you realize that this is the first opportunity I have had to observe a wizard *in situ?* Of course, the magical connections would be clearer if his staff were a little closer."

"You leave that staff where it is," Morwen said. "Fiddle, if either of them tries to go get it, stop them. I don't care how."

"You don't? That's easy, then." Fiddlesticks curled his lips back, showing most of his teeth. "Did I do good? Does this mean I can have fish for dinner?"

"It certainly does," Morwen said. "And possibly a bowl of cream as well. Where's Scorn?"

"With Jasper, watching the staff. Do they get fish, too?"

"Yes, if they want it." Morwen transferred her attention to the six-inch wizard. He had a sharp, angular face half-covered by an untidy brown beard, and he seemed a little young compared to most of the wizards Morwen had met. Not to mention short. "If it won't interfere with your observations, Telemain, I'd like to ask this fellow a few questions."

"Hmmm? Oh, not at all." Telemain did not even glance up.

"Good. Now, wizard, who are you and what are you doing in the Enchanted Forest?"

The wizard drew himself up to his full height, which brought his head about even with Fiddlesticks's nose. "I am Antorell, and if you know what is good for you, you will not meddle with me!" he said in a shrill voice.

"I might have known," Morwen said.

"What's that?" Telemain said, looking up. "Morwen, these readings are absurd. This fellow can't be very good."

Antorell's face turned bright red. Morwen smiled. "He isn't. This is Antorell, Telemain."

"Antorell, Antorell. Oh. The son of Head Wizard Zemenar?"

"That's right," Antorell said. "And you'll regret—"

"Isn't he the one Cimorene keeps melting?" Telemain said. "And shouldn't he be larger?"

Antorell's face became downright purple. Curious about the change, Fiddlesticks leaned forward, and his whiskers brushed the side of Antorell's head. The wizard shrieked and jumped away, the cat pounced, and bits of moss flew in all directions. After a moment, the rapidly moving tangle resolved into Fiddlesticks crouched over the wizard. One front paw, with claws fully extended, rested on each of Antorell's shoulders. Antorell looked terrified.

"He's the one," Morwen said to Telemain. "Very good, Fiddle. You may back up now. I don't think he'll do that again."

"Fascinating," Telemain murmured, his eyes fixed

on the cat. "Did you see the sparks, Morwen? He cast a basic warding-off spell, but it didn't affect the cat at all!"

Morwen frowned in concern. "Fiddlesticks?"

"Well, of course it didn't do anything to me." Fiddlesticks eased slowly off Antorell's chest and sat down very close beside him. "Wizards don't know how to handle cats. I don't think they're very smart."

"Get that beast away from me!" Antorell cried as Fiddlesticks raised a paw and flexed his claws.

"See?" said Fiddlesticks, and began washing wizard germs out from between his toes.

"Calm down," Morwen told Antorell. "Fiddlesticks won't hurt you. Unless I tell him to, of course. What are you doing in the Enchanted Forest?"

"I won't tell you." Antorell was plainly trying to sound defiant, but all he managed was sulky.

"Morwen?" Scorn wound her way around the far edge of the bush. "How long are we going to have to watch this staff? It's not doing anything, and Jasper wants to take a nap."

"I'll be there as soon as we finish with Antorell," Morwen said.

"What is it?" Telemain asked.

"Scorn wants the staff taken care of," Morwen told him. "Antorell—"

"That presents no difficulty," Telemain said. "If you'll just fetch it here, Scorn, I'll do it for you."

Scorn gave him a long look. "*Dogs* fetch." She turned her back and lay down, her tail thrashing indignantly.

"That means 'no,' I take it," Telemain said with a sigh.

"It does. And I told you I didn't want the staff anywhere near the wizard," Morwen said.

"A proper spirit of scientific investigation—"

"I'm more interested in self-preservation. Study the staff later. Antorell—"

"Ha!" said Antorell. "You are too late! Behold!"

With a flourish, he raised his right arm. As he did, he began to glow. Fiddlesticks pulled his head back in surprise, and the glow began pulsing, first bright, then dim. After three pulses, Antorell started growing. He gained an inch on the next pulse, two on the one after that, and then he had grown to a foot in height.

"Bother," said Morwen, and grabbed for the bucket.

"Argelfraster," said Telemain, and pointed at Antorell.

"Eeeaugh!" said Antorell, his expression changing from sinister to shocked. He continued to glow and pulse, but he was no longer getting taller. A puddle of brown goo began to spread out from under his robe where his feet should have been. "No! Help! You can't *do* this to me!"

"Wow!" said Fiddlesticks. "Look at him go!"

Morwen nodded, but she kept the bucket of soapy water ready to throw, just in case. Antorell was now melting faster than he was growing. In another minute, all that was left were his robes and the puddle of goo sinking slowly into the moss. Fiddlesticks edged up to it and sniffed, then backed away rapidly.

"What was all that noise?" Killer said from behind Telemain. "Part of it sounded like another donkey."

"No, it was a wizard, though in this case it's much the same thing," Morwen said. "You needn't worry.

He's gone now." She set her bucket down once more and gave Telemain a nod of approval. "Congratulations. It works."

"Yes, and did you notice the echo effect on the size-amplification spell?" Telemain shook his head. "Remarkable. The theoretical ramifications—"

"Are very interesting, I'm sure," Morwen said. "How permanent is this?" She waved at the gooey robes.

"Not very, I'm afraid," Telemain said. "He'll be back in a day or two."

Killer ambled over to the puddle. "Is this edible?" he asked in a doubtful tone.

"No!" said Morwen and Telemain together.

"What an awful idea," said Fiddlesticks, wrinkling his nose.

"What a mess," said Scorn.

"Don't touch it," Morwen said to Killer. "With two spells on you already, you shouldn't take any chances with wizard residuum."

"Oh," said Killer. He looked at the puddle again and sighed. "But I'm *hungry*. And thirsty. What do donkeys eat?"

"We'll take care of you in a minute or two," Morwen promised. "Finish up quickly, Telemain. We're leaving." Beach or no beach, King Mendanbar and Queen Cimorene had to be found and informed as soon as possible. Morwen started back toward the clover patch to collect her broomstick.

"Don't forget about that staff!" Scorn called after her.

Getting ready to leave didn't take long. Morwen picked up the staff—and Jasper, who was still guarding it—on her way back to Telemain. She noticed with interest that the staff was over three feet long and expanding slowly. Apparently the shrinking spell was wearing off it even without Antorell's help.

When she reached him, Telemain was just stowing the last of his shiny instruments back in one of his pockets. "Have we got everyone?" the magician asked.

"Everyone but the wizard," Scorn said. "And good riddance to *him*, I say."

"Yes," Morwen replied to both Telemain and Scorn. "If you'll take the staff, Telemain—"

"I wouldn't do that," Jasper said, jumping down from Morwen's shoulder.

Morwen paused, frowning, then saw Killer standing by the bucket of soapy water. He lowered his head and sniffed experimentally. "Why not? It smells nice."

"That's the lemon juice," Morwen said.

"It's got *soap* in it," Fiddlesticks said, lashing his tail. "It's for *melting wizards*."

"There aren't any wizards around, and I'm thirsty." Before anyone could stop him, Killer took a large slurp. His ears stood straight up and he reared back, shaking his head. "Blea-eea-eaugh! That tastes terrible."

"Fiddle warned you," said Scorn, with a visible lack of sympathy. "So did Jasper. Serves you right for not listening."

"What's it doing to his nose?" Fiddlesticks said, poking his own nose forward until he had to stand up and follow it. "Look at his nose, Morwen. It's turning blue."

"Not just the nose." Jasper stared in fascination. "His whole face is changing color."

Killer gave a frightened snort and shook his head, sneezing soap bubbles in all directions. The color went on spreading. Soon his head and neck were a bright, clear sky blue that continued to inch up his ears, down his forelegs, and across his back.

"Help!" Killer cried. "Morwen, you're a witch. Make it stop!"

"That would be inadvisable," Telemain said. He, too, was watching Killer's changing color with great interest. "The synergistic action of the original wizardly enchantment, which was itself an unstructured mechanical surplus and therefore liable to produce unpredictable side effects, and the secondary vegetation-based enchantment has rendered you vulnerable to the wizard liquefication fluid while also, fortunately, mitigating its effects."

"What?" said Killer.

"You've got a leftover bit of a wizard's spell on you and you don't know what all it may do. You're lucky you aren't melting, the way the wizard did," Scorn summarized.

"But just *look* at me!"

"I think it's an improvement," Morwen said. "Much better than being blotchy."

"Blue? *Blue* is better than blotchy?" The color had spread to Killer's hindquarters. Only his tail and his back legs were still a patchy white-and-brown.

"Not much," said Scorn.

"Settle it later," Morwen said. "We have to go. Telemain—"

"Everyone still here? Good." Telemain raised a hand and made a circle in the air with his left forefinger.

The wide silver band on his finger sparkled as he said in a low voice,

> *"Convey this crowd*
> *On wind and cloud*
> *To the castle of the King*
> *By the power of this ring."*

On the last word, Telemain clapped his hands together loudly. The trees melted and ran like soft wax on a hot stove. To her surprise, Morwen felt no sensation of movement. It was more as if she were standing still while everything around her shifted. As she nodded in approval, the blur flowed into a new shape and solidified.

They now stood on the paving stones of the castle courtyard, in the relatively narrow strip between the moat and the main door. A large dragon lay along the left side of the castle, basking in the sun. Her head, with the three stubby horns that proclaimed her a female, rested at the edge of the moat; most of her body was hidden by a tower with two staircases running around its outside. Her wings were partway open to catch the sun, and her green scales glittered, even where they were beginning to turn gray at the edges.

"Eee-augh!" Killer brayed in terror. "A dragon!"

"Oh, good," Morwen said at the same moment. "That will save some time."

"Good?" Killer seemed to be trying to hide behind Telemain and to watch the dragon at the same time. "A *dragon* is good?"

"Not *a* dragon, you idiot," said Scorn. "That's Kazul, the *King* of the Dragons."

Killer edged away. "Does he eat rabbits? Or donkeys?"

"*She* prefers cherries jubilee," Jasper said.

"She?" Killer looked thoroughly confused, as well as alarmed. "But—the 'King of the Dragons'?"

" 'King of the Dragons' is the name of a job," Jasper said. "It has nothing to do with gender."

"Dragons are very sensible about things like that," Fiddlesticks put in, nodding. "Almost as sensible as me. But they don't like fish."

"I'd be happier if they didn't like donkeys."

"Don't worry about King Kazul," Morwen said to Killer. "She doesn't eat friends of friends."

"Not even if she's hungry?" Killer's ears pricked forward nervously. "She looks hungry to me."

Before Morwen could respond, the castle door creaked open. From the dark hallway inside, a voice called, "Madame Morwen! Magician Telemain! Welcome to the castle."

6

In Which the Plot Positively Curdles, and the King of the Dragons Loses her Temper

As everyone turned to look, a three-foot elf wearing a gold lace collar and a crisp white shirt under a green velvet coat with gold buttons, white silk hose, and green shoes with chunky gold heels stepped into view in the doorway of the castle. "Welcome, all of you," he added, bowing low.

"Hello, Willin," Morwen said. "We need to see King Mendanbar and Queen Cimorene right away."

"In regard to what?" the elf asked.

"Technical difficulties," Telemain said. "We have discovered a possible disruption in the obstructive enchantment fabricated by King Mendanbar and myself, and—"

"Er, yes, of course," said Willin. "I'll tell the King immediately. You needn't give me the details."

Telemain caught Morwen's eye and winked. Morwen suppressed a smile and said, "And while we're waiting, Killer's hungry." She nodded at the donkey. "If your kitchen could put something together that would suit him . . ."

"Certainly," Willin said. "Just trot around back, er, Killer, and the cook will take care of you." He waved toward the left, where Kazul was sleeping.

"I'm not *that* hungry!" Killer said.

"Go around the other way, then," Morwen told him. "It doesn't really matter. Just *go*."

"I'll show him!" Fiddlesticks bounded across to Killer. "The kitchen is this way. They have cream, and butter, and fish, and . . ." His voice faded as they rounded the crooked tower by the stone bridge.

Scorn stood up and stretched. "What a pair of idiots." She looked at Jasper. "Maybe we should go after them and make sure they don't get into trouble."

"An excellent idea," Jasper agreed. With an air of determined casualness, the two cats strolled off, following the donkey.

Willin looked after them with a worried frown. "Did I offend them?"

"Not at all," Morwen assured him. When his expression did not clear, she added, "They're hoping the cook will give them some cream. Now, we'll just go have a word with Kazul while you let Cimorene know we're here. Oh, and would you put this bucket somewhere? I've enough to carry without it."

"Very good, ma'am," Willin said stiffly. He accepted the bucket and vanished into the castle, closing the door carefully behind him.

"Morwen, Mendanbar's the one we really need to see," Telemain said softly. "King Kazul—"

"Has good reason to be just as interested in the doings of wizards as the rest of us," Morwen said. "Besides, it wouldn't be polite to go in without at least saying hello."

"I suppose not," Telemain said, and the two walked across the courtyard to talk to the dragon. Up close, Kazul was an even more impressive dragon than she looked from a distance. Standing, she was at least six times Morwen's height, even without her wings, and every inch was muscle and armor scales. The sleepy, contented expression on her face vanished as Morwen and Telemain drew nearer, and by the time they were close enough to talk, the dragon was wide awake and ready for them.

"Hello, Morwen, Telemain," Kazul said. "Wizards again?" She flicked a claw in the direction of the staff Morwen held.

"Hello, Kazul," Morwen said. "It's *a* wizard, at least."

"I thought you'd shut them out of the forest," Kazul said to Telemain.

"What one magician can do, another can find a way around," Telemain said with a shrug. "Unless the quantity of energy involved reaches a magnitude that renders—"

Kazul cleared her throat pointedly. Telemain stopped. "Unless *what?*" asked the dragon.

"Um. Unless you . . . put so much power into a spell that nobody can, er, examine it closely enough to, um, figure out how to break it without getting fried by the backlash," Telemain said carefully.

"Ah. Well, I suppose nothing's perfect."

A bell chimed, and all three turned to look at the castle. The door swung open, and Willin marched out. "Their Majesties King Mendanbar and Queen Cimorene of the Enchanted Forest," he announced, and bowed low.

"Hello, Morwen, Telemain. We were just trying to get you on the magic mirror." The speaker was a tall young woman in a loose cream-colored shirt and a pair of baggy gray pants tucked into short leather boots. Her black braids were wound around and around her head like a crown, and her face was both lovely and intelligent.

As she came down the steps and into the courtyard, a man emerged from the door behind her. He was equally tall and dark-haired, and he wore a plain gold circlet that he had pushed back off his forehead. It gave him a rakish look.

"Yes, the gargoyle said something about wizards," the man said, coming forward. "Is it urgent?"

"Important, certainly," Morwen said. "Urgent, possibly. I don't think it's an emergency. Not yet. Hello, Cimorene, Mendanbar."

There was a brief round of greeting, and then Mendanbar said, "I thought something was wrong in the forest. It's been niggling at me ever since we got home."

Cimorene frowned. "You didn't say anything."

"I didn't want to worry you."

Cimorene rolled her eyes. "Mendanbar, I haven't suddenly turned to glass just because I'm going to have a baby."

"Well, but—"

"I believe that can wait," Morwen interrupted tactfully. "The wizards shouldn't."

"Yes, now that we're all here, tell us where you came across *that*." Kazul waved at the wizard's staff in Morwen's right hand.

Morwen nodded and launched into a summary of the events following Killer's appearance in her back garden. Cimorene, Mendanbar, and Kazul listened without interrupting, though their expressions grew more and more serious. When she finished, Mendanbar turned to Telemain.

"These dead spots. I thought the spell we worked out prevented them."

"It should have," Telemain said, nodding. "And since the spell has worked perfectly well for over a year, it seems unlikely that the breakdown is due to an inherent flaw; nonetheless, I think the initial phase of our investigation should involve an examination and analysis of the primary linkages."

Cimorene blinked and looked at Mendanbar.

"He doesn't think there should be anything wrong with the spell, but he wants to check and make sure," Mendanbar translated. "In that case, we'll need the sword, won't we? I'll go get it." He snapped his fingers, and a small gold key materialized out of the air in front of him and dropped into his hand. An instant later, Mendanbar and the key vanished. A quiet huff of air rushed in to fill the space he had vacated.

"Now *that* is a transportation spell that has everything," Telemain said with a touch of envy. "Power, elegance, and economy of style. I wish I could determine exactly how he does it."

"*I* wish he could get it to work properly outside the Enchanted Forest," said Cimorene. "It would make visiting Kazul much easier."

"A little walking in the mountains is good for you," Kazul said.

Cimorene looked at the dragon with fond exasperation. "It may be a little walk to *you*, but it takes a good deal longer for *us*. And as I recall, you usually fly most of the way. You shouldn't give advice you don't follow."

"When I was your age, I did follow it."

"When you were Cimorene's age, you were a rambunctious dragonet barely out of the egg," Morwen said. "None of which has anything to do with our present problems."

Air puffed outward as Mendanbar reappeared. His face was set in grim lines and his hands were empty. "It's gone," he said. "The lock on the chest has been melted to a puddle, the lid is up, and the sword is gone. And there are tangles of wizard magic all over the armory. It'll take me a week to straighten them out."

There was a moment of stunned silence. Then Kazul made a low growling sound and a small flame flickered around her jaws. Cimorene's eyes went wide and she stepped quickly in front of Mendanbar, muttering something under her breath as she moved.

Probably the fire-proofing spell she discovered when she was Kazul's princess, Morwen thought. *I hope it still works.* Dropping the wizard's staff, Morwen grabbed Telemain's arm and hauled him forward.

"Morwen, what are you—"

Kazul sat back on her haunches, snapped open her wings, and roared, sending bright streams of fire shooting across the courtyard. The flames missed Telemain's head by inches, and the near edge engulfed Cimorene and Mendanbar.

"Kazul, stop that immediately!" Cimorene cried from the center of the fire. She didn't sound as if she were in pain, so the fire-proofing spell must be working.

"Yes, you don't want to finish those wizards' work for them," Morwen said as loudly as she could. "And I'm sure they'd be delighted if you roasted the King and Queen of the Enchanted Forest for them."

The roaring and the flames did not stop, but Kazul tilted her head so that the stream of fire shot harmlessly up into the air. As the flames lifted away from Cimorene and Mendanbar, Morwen breathed a sigh of relief. Cimorene's creamy shirt was now closer in color to toast, and the ends of Mendanbar's hair had crinkled visibly from the heat, but they both seemed unhurt. They ran forward to join Morwen and Telemain next to Kazul's right shoulder. Windows were flying open and closed all over the castle as people looked out to find out what all the noise was and then quickly ducked back inside.

"I've never seen her like this before, not even when the wizards kidnapped her!" Cimorene shouted over the roaring.

"I hope I never see her like this again!" Mendanbar shouted back. "I'd have been roasted if it hadn't been for that fire-proofing spell of yours. It's a good thing you're so tall."

"Fire-proofing spell?" Telemain lowered his hands from his ears and leaned forward. "What fire-proofing spell? Why hasn't anyone mentioned this before?"

"Later, Telemain," Morwen yelled.

Finally, Kazul paused for breath. In the sudden silence, Cimorene yelled, "Kazul! For goodness' sake, calm down!"

"I will not calm down!" Kazul said, but at least now she was shouting and not breathing fire indiscriminately. "This time the Society of Wizards has gone too far, and I'm not settling for throwing them out of the Enchanted Forest or limiting their power. *This* time I'm going to see the end of them, I swear I am, even if it takes two centuries. By my fire, I swear it!"

"Ah, Kazul." Mendanbar tapped one of the dragon's shoulder scales. "It's *my* sword they've stolen."

"Yes," Cimorene said, "and the first thing we have to do is get it back. The Enchanted Forest needs it."

"Very well," said Kazul. "You may help me exterminate the Society of Wizards." Slowly, she settled back to the ground, scales rattling faintly as she let her wings close.

"First things first," Morwen said. "Cimorene's right; we have to get the sword back, and quickly. Otherwise, the Society of Wizards can walk into the Enchanted Forest and soak up pieces of it until there's nothing left."

"That's probably why they took it," Cimorene said.

"No, no," Telemain put in. "The sword is only *one* of the primary foci. Its physical removal does not invalidate . . ." He paused, glanced at Kazul, and cleared his throat. "Ah, that is, the King's sword just helps maintain the spell. Taking the sword out of the forest doesn't destroy the whole spell. It just weakens it. That's why the dead spots Morwen showed me didn't fill in right away. But the spell is still strong enough to keep the wizards from gobbling up large chunks of the forest."

"Does that mean that if we recover the sword, the forest will be fully protected again?" Mendanbar asked.

Telemain nodded.

"Good. Give me a minute or two to explain to Willin, and I'll be ready to go."

"Go?" Telemain blinked. "But—"

With a huff of air, Mendanbar vanished.

"But what?" asked Cimorene.

"Mendanbar shouldn't go anywhere right now," Morwen said. "It's bad enough that the sword's missing, but no one will know about that for a while unless we tell them. But if the King of the Enchanted Forest goes tearing off on a quest while mysterious things are happening in the forest, people are bound to notice."

"There's more to it than that," Telemain said. "Mendanbar *can't* go after the sword, not if he wants to keep what's left of the antiwizard spell working. He's the other main focus."

"Oh, dear." Cimorene looked back toward the castle, and her lips twitched. "He's not going to like that at all."

"I'm certain that Morwen, Telemain, and I will be able to handle it," Kazul said.

Cimorene frowned. "Don't *you* start fussing at me, Kazul. I'm perfectly capable of—"

"I'm sure you are," Morwen said. "But the Queen of the Enchanted Forest shouldn't go tearing off any more than the King should. You have responsibilities."

"Bother my responsibilities!"

"If I thought you meant that, I'd be worried."

"Retrieving the sword is much more important than anything else I have to do right now. Thank goodness it won't be hard to find."

Morwen frowned, puzzled. "Why do you say that?"

"Well, the wizards have taken it out of the forest, haven't they? Otherwise Telemain's antiwizard spell would still be working." Cimorene smiled briefly at Telemain. "The last time that sword was outside the forest, it started leaking magic the minute it crossed the border."

"Leaking magic?"

Cimorene shrugged. "I don't know what else to call it. And it gets worse and worse the longer the sword is outside the forest. By the end of the week, anyone with any magical ability at all will be able to find that sword with his eyes closed."

"I don't think we can afford to wait that long," Telemain said slowly.

"What? Why not?" Cimorene looked at the magician in alarm. "You don't think the Society of Wizards will try to destroy it, do you?"

"It's not that." Telemain began to pace up and down beside Kazul. "It's the magic leakage. I'd forgotten about it, and of course it didn't matter as long as the sword was inside the forest, but now—"

"Now the wizards have it," Morwen said. "And wizards' staffs absorb magic. If they absorb all the magic the sword leaks, and the leak keeps growing, it won't be long before they're more than we can handle."

"That, too," Telemain said, nodding. "But the real

problem is the source of the magic the sword leaks."

"The source—oh. Oh, dear." Morwen looked at Telemain. "You mean the Enchanted Forest itself?"

Slowly, Telemain nodded again. "I'm afraid so. Mendanbar and I linked the sword directly to the heart of the forest's magic. The defensive enchantment will inhibit the, er, leakage for a while, but after a few days—"

"—the pressure will build up and the sword will start leaking. And all the magic of the Enchanted Forest will drain out of the sword," Morwen finished.

"But that will kill the forest!" Cimorene said. "We have to get that sword back right away."

"Not quite," Kazul said. A thread of smoke continued to trickle angrily out of the corner of her mouth, but otherwise she seemed to be in complete control of herself again. "From what Telemain said, it will take another day or two for the sword to start leaking. Right?"

Telemain nodded. "As near as I can tell."

"Then we don't have to learn to fly by jumping off a cliff. There are still a few things I want to know before we go chasing off."

"Such as?" Morwen asked.

"How the Society of Wizards got inside the castle to steal the sword without anyone noticing, whether they're likely to be back soon, and what we can do about it if they are."

Morwen, Telemain, and Cimorene looked at each other. Then Telemain looked at Kazul. "Commendably methodical. And now that you mention it, I'd better teach all of you the wizard-liquefying spell before we leave."

"You mean you've come up with a better way of melting wizards than soapy water with lemon juice in it?" Cimorene's smile was only a little forced. "Wonderful!"

"I don't know that it's *better*," Telemain said. "However, it appears to have the same effect, requires far less preparation, and is considerably more portable."

"He melted Antorell with it," Morwen said.

Kazul shook herself and stood up. "Enjoy the lesson. I'm going to ask your cook to pack us something for dinner."

"Don't you want to know how to melt wizards?" Cimorene said.

"No." Kazul smiled fiercely, showing all her sharp, silver teeth. "If I run into any wizards, I'm going to eat them."

"Then why are you bothering about dinner?" Telemain asked, frowning.

Kazul's smile broadened. "That's for the rest of you," she said, and glided off.

7

In Which Killer Rises in the World

Mendanbar returned just as Telemain began his explanation of the wizard-melting spell. "You'll want to know this, too, Mendanbar," Telemain said, and went right on with his lecture. The enchantment was typical of the magician's spare spells: it required a lot of preparation and a complicated ritual to set it up, but once that had been done, you could use it several times simply by pointing and saying a trigger word. According to Telemain, you didn't even have to *say* the trigger word aloud.

"Theoretically, a mental recitation would be just as effective," Telemain said. "This theory, however, remains unverified, as no opportunity for experimentation has—"

"Telemain, if you don't stop babbling gobbledygook, I'm going to bring Kazul back to listen," Morwen said. "Mendanbar and I know what you're saying, but Cimorene hasn't the slightest idea what you're talking about."

"Yes, and I'd appreciate it if somebody would translate that last bit," Cimorene said. "It sounded important."

"Just thinking the trigger word ought to be as good as saying it," Mendanbar explained. "But he doesn't know for sure because he hasn't had a chance to test it on a wizard yet."

"Well, you'll probably get one soon," Cimorene said. "Have we got all the ingredients you need for the ritual? Because I think everyone ought to be prepared to melt wizards before anyone goes sword hunting. It's all very well for Kazul to say she'll eat them, but if they have any dragonsbane . . ."

"Good idea," Mendanbar said. "What will we need?"

"I brought the rarer components with me," Telemain said. "If you have seven lemons, a book that's missing half its cover, and three pints of unicorn water, I can start working on it at once."

Mendanbar pursed his lips. "I don't think we have any unicorn water."

"Yes, we do," said Cimorene. "It's in the cupboard by the buckets, in a jug marked 'Magic-Mirror Cleaner.' Don't look at me like that. It was the safest place I could think of. Ever since we put the gargoyle in charge of answering the mirror, nobody but me dares to clean it."

Mendanbar laughed. "I don't blame them."

"Why don't you and Telemain check the library

and start setting up in the Grand Hall?" Cimorene suggested. "Morwen and I will get the other ingredients and meet you there."

The two men agreed to this plan, and the group split up. As the castle door closed, Cimorene gave a sigh of relief.

"How do you stand it?" she asked Morwen.

"The way Telemain complicates things when he talks?" Morwen shook her head. "I don't have to, much."

"I thought you were old friends."

"We are. That doesn't mean we see a lot of each other, though I'll admit that he drops by much more often now that he lives in the Enchanted Forest, too."

"Even so . . ."

Morwen thought for a minute. "The only thing you can do is avoid talking about magic with him," she said at last. "He's reasonably clear when it comes to normal conversation, but as soon as anyone mentions spells he gets technical. Or you could make sure Kazul is always with you."

"Yes, I'd noticed that Telemain doesn't—"

A distant bray interrupted Cimorene in midsentence. "Good heavens," she said. "What on earth was that?"

"Killer," Morwen said, walking more quickly. "Unless you've acquired a donkey since the last time I was here."

"A donkey? No, but—"

As they rounded the last corner and came in sight of the kitchen, Cimorene stopped short. The cook stood in the half-open kitchen door, brandishing a copper frying pan to keep Killer from forcing his way inside, while Scorn and Jasper watched from the safety of a nearby window ledge. Midway between the kitchen and the moat, Kazul sat on her haunches, smiling down at the terrified blue donkey in amusement. Since the smile showed a fair number of teeth, it wasn't helping Killer's state of mind at all.

"Killer," Morwen said sternly. "Stop that this instant."

"But it's a *dragon!*" Killer wailed. "And it's *right there!* Eee-augh!"

The cook glanced toward them, gasped, and dropped the frying pan. "Your Majesty!"

Taking full advantage of the cook's distraction, Killer flung himself forward. He hit the door with a thud, shoving it wide and knocking the cook over backward. As his head and front feet disappeared inside the kitchen, a cat yowled loudly in surprise and pain.

"Fiddlesticks!" Morwen said. "That does it." She raised her arms.

> *"Sky and sea and whirling sands,*
> *Stop that creature where he stands!"*

On the final word, she brought both hands down in a swift chopping gesture. Killer stopped moving and gave a startled bellow. An instant later, Fiddlesticks shot out from between the donkey's legs. Morwen breathed a quiet sigh of relief.

"He stepped on my *tail!*" Fiddlesticks said with great indignation. He sat down at Kazul's feet and began energetically washing the offended part.

"I'm surprised it wasn't your nose," Scorn said. "You poke it into enough peculiar places."

"Help! Hee-eeau-elp!" Killer cried. "I'm going to be eaten!"

"Get this creature out of my kitchen!" the cook yelled as he scrambled to his feet.

"Quiet, all of you," said Cimorene, edging her way through the narrow gap between Killer's rear end and the door frame. Since Fiddlesticks seemed more or less unharmed, Morwen followed Cimorene inside. Killer continued to moan and whimper despite Cimorene's order, but he at least stopped braying.

Inside, Cimorene glanced around the kitchen, which was nearly as clean and tidy as Morwen's, and nodded to the cook. The cook bowed deeply. Cimorene turned to Killer. "Nobody is going to eat anyone here unless I say so. Now, how did this happen?"

"Just how you'd expect," Scorn said from the window. "Killer was being stupid again."

"I'm not stupid," Killer said. "Eee-eeaugh! Oh, help!"

"I said *quiet*," Cimorene said.

"But I can't move, and there's a dragon—"

"I can arrange it so you can't talk, either," Morwen said. "And if you don't start behaving yourself, I'll do it. Cimorene, this is Killer. He ought to be a rabbit of the usual size and color, but he's had some trouble with wizards lately. This is Cimorene, the Queen of the Enchanted Forest. I think you should answer her question."

Killer rolled his eyes and waggled his ears, managing to look foolish and terrified at the same time, but after a few more minutes of reassurance, coaxing, and stern commands, he calmed down enough to explain. He had been waiting for the castle cook to mix up his promised lunch, and hadn't noticed Kazul's arrival. When the cats pointed her out to him, he had been nervous, but he hadn't really started to worry until Kazul asked the cook to pack provisions for a journey. What had really panicked him, though, had been the dragon saying, in answer to a question from the cook, that the provisions should be for human people only, because she would find her own meals.

"There, you see?" Scorn said, lashing her tail. "He was being stupid."

"I can see why it might make you nervous," Cimorene said to Killer. "Kazul can be a bit intimidating up close." She considered for a moment. "Kazul won't eat you once you've been properly introduced. Let him loose, Morwen, and I'll take him over and present him."

"Are you sure?" Killer asked.

"Positive," Cimorene told him. "Dragons are very polite. Morwen?"

Since all the cats were out of danger and Killer seemed to have settled down, Morwen nodded agreement. Bringing her hands together at waist height, she said,

"Fire and cloud and rain and snow,
Lift the spell and let him go!"

As she spoke, she raised her arms in a slow reversal of the movement she had used to freeze Killer where he stood.

For a long moment, nothing seemed to happen. Morwen frowned, wondering if the wizards' size-changing spell was interfering with her witchcraft.

Then a ripple ran across Killer's back, like heat rising from an iron stove. He shivered, shook himself, and pranced backward several steps, ducking his head to clear the top of the doorway.

"Thanks," he said. "Um, could we just sort of skip the part about presenting me to the dragon for now?"

"That wouldn't be a good—Killer, are you growing again?" Morwen asked. "You look taller."

Jasper yawned widely and jumped down from the window ledge. "He's not taller," the cat said, strolling forward. "He's just farther up."

Automatically, Morwen, Cimorene, and the cook glanced down, following Jasper's movement. Morwen blinked. Between Killer's front hooves and the flagstones of the courtyard stretched a long inch of empty air.

"I wonder if he'll still leave footprints?" Cimorene said, half to herself.

"What is it?" Killer asked nervously. "What are you all staring at?" He looked down and his ears stiffened. "Eee-augh!" He pranced backward, out of sight, and Cimorene and Morwen hurried out after him. With every step, he gained a little more height, until he was a good four inches above the ground. "Help! I'm falling!"

"You're not falling," Scorn said. "You're floating."

"He is, isn't he?" Fiddlesticks said, walking over. "And it's a very good idea. He can't step on anybody's tail now."

"Hold still," Morwen said to the donkey. "Every time you take a step, you get farther up. If you keep moving, you'll be over the castle in no time. And if the spell suddenly wears off . . ."

"Eee-augh!" Killer rolled his eyes and planted his feet firmly in thin air. "Now what?"

"Now you wait," Morwen told him. "This looks like another side effect of mixing different kinds of magic, and that's really Telemain's specialty. I'll send him out as soon as we're done inside."

"Tell him to hurry!"

Cimorene shook her head. "I'm afraid it will take a while, but we'll bring him as soon as we can. In the meantime, Evim will get you some lunch." She looked back over her shoulder at the cook, who nodded and vanished into the kitchen.

Behind Killer, scales scraped noisily against stone. "This is very entertaining," Kazul said, "but haven't we got more important things to do than argue with an oversized blue donkey with avian ambitions?"

Killer rolled his eyes and choked back another bray. Cimorene smiled but shook her head. "It's not quite as silly as it looks. Kazul, this is Killer; Killer, this is Kazul, the King of the Dragons. Killer is the one who found out that the wizards are back in the forest, Kazul."

"He is?" Kazul came around in front, where she could see Killer more clearly. "Have you got any idea how they got into the palace?"

"N-no, sir—I mean, ma'am," said Killer.

"The size-changing spell must have had something to do with it," Morwen said. "If they shrank themselves small enough to sneak through the door without being seen—"

"That would be hard," Cimorene said. "Our regular doorman is on vacation, so Willin's been handling it. And he's not all that big himself. Those wizards would have had to shrink awfully small to get past him."

"There are other doors," Kazul pointed out. "This one, for instance." She waved a claw at the kitchen entrance.

"Yes, but there's a spell on them that rings a bell in the footman's room whenever someone who doesn't belong here comes through one of them."

"However they did it, we aren't going to figure it out standing here," Morwen said. "Either we should go down to the armory and investigate, or we should get those lemons and go meet Mendanbar and Telemain the way we planned."

"Good heavens, I almost forgot," Cimorene said. "Lemons and unicorn water it is. I'm sorry, Kazul, but we can't do everything at once."

Cimorene and Morwen said good-bye to Kazul and went back into the kitchen, where they collected the lemons and unicorn water. Just as they were leaving, Jasper slipped out from behind a large basket of apples that was leaning against a corner wall.

"Morwen?" said the cat. "I've got something to tell you."

"All right," Morwen said. "Would you mind waiting a minute, Cimorene? Jasper wants to talk to me, and he wouldn't interrupt if it weren't important."

"Of course," Cimorene said. "But do try to be quick, Jasper. We've already taken more time than we should have."

Jasper favored Cimorene with a slow blink of approval. "I like her. She understands cats better than most people do."

"Very likely," said Morwen. "Now, what was it you wanted to tell me?"

"I know how the wizards got into the armory."

"Well?"

The cat coughed and looked around to make sure none of the other animals were within hearing distance. "Plumbing and mouse holes," he said very softly. "There's an old drain that goes under the moat and comes out in the forest. The wizards used it to get into the castle and then wandered around in the walls until they found a mouse hole into the armory. Once they had the sword, they used a transport spell to leave."

"How do you know all this?"

Jasper hunched his shoulders in embarrassment. "I asked the castle mice. A couple of them are friends of mine, and they gave me the whole story. Don't tell anyone, will you? If Scorn finds out, I'll never hear the end of it."

"If Scorn or anyone else says one word about it, you let me know," Morwen said. "That was very well done, Jasper. Thank you."

Jasper raised his chin and arched his back proudly. "You're welcome. But I'd still rather you didn't tell Scorn."

"I won't," Morwen promised. "All right, Cimorene. Let's go."

"What was that about?" Cimorene asked as they left the kitchen.

"Jasper found out how the wizards got in," Morwen said, and explained as well as she could without mentioning Jasper's friendship with the mice.

Cimorene frowned. "Mouse holes? That's awful. We'll never find them all, and even if we did, the mice would just make new ones. And no one has *ever* invented a spell to keep mice out. Not one that works, anyway."

"And if you can't keep the mice out, you can't keep the wizards out, either. It's a problem." Morwen thought for a minute. "Why don't you ask the mice to help?"

"Ask the mice?" Cimorene looked startled, then nodded. "Of course. Even if they won't tell us where their holes are, they can let us know if any more wizards try to use them. But who should we get to talk to them?"

"Your gargoyle. I'll wager my best broomstick that the mice will talk to him, and Telemain can rig up some portable magic mirrors so he can warn you when you're in other parts of the castle."

"Can Telemain make portable magic mirrors?"

"I don't know," Morwen said. "But we can ask."

They turned down the last long corridor that led to the Grand Hall, and Morwen's eyes widened. "Impressive," she said after a moment.

"Haven't you been to the Grand Hall before?" Cimorene said.

"No," Morwen said positively. "I'd remember."

The door to the Grand Hall was made of gold. It was twice as wide and three times as tall as a normal door, and it was covered with relief patterns that moved and twisted if you looked at them too long. Cimorene smiled at Morwen, tapped at the door with one finger, and waited. After a moment, the door swung smoothly open.

"We're here," Cimorene said, stepping forward. "Are you ready to start?"

8

In Which Telemain Does a Spell and Morwen Misses a Call

The Grand Hall was as large as a ballroom, with a high ceiling and a green marble floor. Sunlight streamed through a dozen windows in the upper half of the walls, and two branches of unlit candles hung below each window, ready for evening or a cloudy day. Mendanbar and Telemain had pushed the few pieces of furniture—five high-backed wooden chairs and a long low-backed couch—up against the far wall. In the empty center of the room, Telemain had set up a large iron brazier, about three feet high and nearly five feet across.

"Where on earth did you get that?" Cimorene asked.

"I ordered it from the dwarfs," Telemain said, stooping to squint across the rim of the brazier. "And

I had to send it back twice. The wizard liquefication spell requires extraordinary precision in the initial stages." With considerable difficulty, he shoved the brazier half an inch to the right and stooped to check its position once more.

"I made a quick trip to his house just now to bring it," Mendanbar said. "I don't need the sword for a spell that simple."

Cimorene smiled at him. "Thank you. How long will this take?"

"Not long," Telemain said, rising. "You've got the lemons and the unicorn water?"

Morwen handed them to him. "I don't think I've seen a setup quite like this before. How did you think of it?"

"The design was not difficult, once the theoretical basis for the spell was determined." Telemain carefully set the lemons on the floor and opened the bottle of unicorn water. It glowed with a faint silver-white light as he poured it into the brazier. "The efficacy of the cleansing solution in liquefying wizards suggested the operation of an antithetical principle, which—"

"Did you have to get him started?" Cimorene asked reproachfully.

"Yes," said Morwen. "I want to know how this works. Talk to Mendanbar, if you'd rather not listen."

From one of his many pockets, Telemain produced a small envelope. As he mixed and poured and arranged the various elements of the spell, he explained each procedure in detail. Morwen was impressed in spite of herself. The spell was clearly a major magical achievement.

Finally the preparations were finished and the brazier was half-full of white, foamy liquid. "That's enough," Telemain said. "Now, would all of you come here and hold your right hands over the brazier, please." Frowning, he watched the bubbling liquid until the foam reached the lip of the brazier. Then he said,

"Over and under, in and out.
Back and through and roundabout.
Send them away when we wish them to go.
Argelfraster!"

The liquid spattered upward as if someone had thrown a large rock into it. Three icy droplets fell on Morwen's extended hand, and several more sprinkled her robe and glasses. It was all she could do not to flinch. Then, with a burbling hiss like a giant steam bubble bursting, the liquid exploded into a dense white cloud and rolled over them. The clean parts of Morwen's glasses fogged up immediately. Beside her, she heard Mendanbar cough.

"That's right, take a deep breath." Telemain's voice sounded very far away. Somewhere in the thick fog, Cimorene gasped and started coughing.

Warily, Morwen sniffed. The fog was bitterly cold and smelled strongly of lemons and bleach. "Bother," she muttered, and breathed in as Telemain had directed. As she had expected, she began to cough. A moment later, the fog cleared.

"Very good," Telemain said, beaming at the three of them as they gasped for air. "You can put your hands down now."

"You might have warned us," Cimorene said when she could talk again.

"About what?" Telemain sounded genuinely puzzled.

"Any number of things," Morwen said, taking off her glasses. Concentrating briefly, she reached into her sleeve, pulled out a clean handkerchief, and carefully wiped the lenses. "The temperature of that concoction, the fact that we were supposed to breathe that steam, and the presence of bleach in the mixture, for example."

"Why the bleach?" Mendanbar asked, in a tone nearly as puzzled as Telemain's.

Morwen settled her glasses back on her nose and scowled at Telemain. "Take a good look at my robe." She held out her arms so that he could clearly see all the pale purple-gray dots where his magic fluid had spattered across the black fabric.

"I'm sorry, Morwen," Telemain said. "I didn't realize it would do that."

"Obviously." Tucking her handkerchief into her sleeve, Morwen shook her head. "At least the spell worked."

"You're sure?" Cimorene asked. "I didn't feel anything when it went off. Except like coughing."

"An unfortunate but necessary side effect," Telemain said, nodding. "It may be possible to eliminate the discomfort in the future, but this time I thought it best to use a proven method."

"Didn't you have to adjust for the number of people involved?" Morwen asked.

"A simple matter of altering the balance of ingredients," Telemain assured her.

"And the trigger word is *argelfraster?*" Morwen went on. "For all of us?"

Telemain nodded. "Say it, or think it very clearly,

and point your finger at the wizard. It's quite effective."

"How did you pick a word like *argelfraster?*" Cimorene asked.

"I wanted something memorable."

"It is that," Morwen murmured. "Telemain, if you are quite finished, I am going home. I want to change clothes and make arrangements with the cats before I go sword hunting. Oh, and take a look at Killer before you leave, or he's likely to float off and starve."

"Float off?"

Cimorene shook her head. "Morwen, in your own way you can be just as bad as he is. It's like this, Telemain . . ." She began explaining what had happened in and around the kitchen.

Frowning, Mendanbar moved closer to Morwen. "I understand why you want to stop at your house before we leave," he said, "and I know you can get yourself back there somehow—"

"I have my broom with me," Morwen said. "It's outside, by the front door where we arrived."

Mendanbar nodded. "Still, I'd like to get this expedition under way as fast as I can. If I send you home on a quick spell, you'll get there much sooner than if you fly."

"That would be fine, as long as you're willing to send my cats and my broom with me," Morwen said. "And make sure someone remembers about Killer. He's a nuisance, but it isn't his fault that he's turned into a six-foot blue floating donkey. Well, mostly it isn't."

"Of course." Mendanbar's eyes got a faraway look, as they always did when he was drawing on the magic of the Enchanted Forest. His right hand moved, as if he were plucking a string, and Fiddlesticks, Jasper, and

Scorn appeared on the green marble in front of Morwen. All three were crouched around a bowl-sized circle, and Fiddlesticks had cream on his nose.

"Hey!" said Fiddlesticks. "I wasn't *finished!*"

"I'll give you something more when we get home," Morwen said. "I believe that's everyone, Mendanbar."

"I'll see you later, then," Mendanbar said, and raised his hand. "Telemain and Kazul and I will meet you at your house. We won't be long." His fingers twitched and the room started to fade.

As the walls blurred into gray mist, Morwen heard Telemain say, "Ah, about this expedition, Mendanbar, I don't think . . ." His voice grew faint and faraway, then was swallowed in the mist. A moment later, the mist cleared, leaving Morwen standing in the large open area in front of her house.

"Remarkably convenient," Morwen said, bending to pick up her broom.

"He could have set us on the porch, if he'd wanted to." Jasper strolled forward and paused at the foot of the steps. "Do you need me for anything now, Morwen?"

"I didn't mean the transportation," Morwen said. "I was referring to the timing. And no, I won't need you for a while."

"Then I'll just take a nap until you do. All this running around is exhausting." Jasper vanished under the porch.

"What timing?" Fiddlesticks asked. "Do you mean it's time for some fish?"

"No, I mean that I won't have to help explain to Mendanbar why he can't leave the Enchanted Forest to look for his sword." Morwen walked briskly up the steps and set her broom against the wall next to the door, where it would be handy. "Scorn, please get everyone together in the garden in about half an hour."

"Half an hour? I thought you were in a hurry."

"We are, but it'll take at least that long for Cimorene and Telemain to convince Mendanbar that he can't go. Run along, now. I've got to pack." With that, Morwen pushed open the front door and went inside.

Slightly less than half an hour later, Morwen walked out the back door into the garden. The sleeves of the bleach-speckled robe had been emptied and disenchanted, and the robe itself dumped into the rag basket. She had transferred the sleeve spell to her new robe (identical to the old one, except for the bleach speckles) and packed both sleeves with magic supplies and a variety of everyday items that might come in handy, including several lemons, a small collapsible bucket, and a bottle of liquid soap. Spells or no spells, Morwen did not intend to take unnecessary chances. Since she did not know how long they would be gone, she added an extra robe, a blanket, and several chicken-salad sandwiches. She considered putting in a few bottles of cider as well, but there were limits to what the spell would hold, and her sleeves were growing heavy, a sure sign that the limits were close.

The cats had already collected in the garden, lolling in patches of sun, perching in the branches of the largest apple tree, or stalking along the garden rows, as if they had all intended to be there for reasons of their own. Smiling slightly, Morwen sat down on the back step next to Miss Eliza. In a few minutes, the other cats drifted over to join them.

"I'm glad you're all here," Morwen told them. "There's been some trouble, and there'll probably be more."

"Scorn and Jasper told us," Murgatroyd said. "Wizards."

"Revolting creatures," Miss Eliza said.

"I'll kill one for you, if you want," Trouble offered.

"I don't think that will be necessary," Morwen said. "Telemain and I hope to retrieve the King's sword and put a stop to this nonsense once and for all. Trouble and Scorn will come with me. The rest of you will stay here and guard the house and garden."

"How long will you be gone?" Aunt Ophelia asked.

"I'm not sure. At least a week, I expect, unless we're very lucky."

"You should take us all," Chaos said, crouching and lashing his tail fiercely. "You might need us. Wizards are tough."

"Hah," said Trouble. "Wizards aren't tough. You just have to know the right place to dig in your claws. Ogres, now, ogres are—"

"We are well aware of your talents, Trouble," said Miss Eliza. "This is not the time to brag."

"I would prefer that you stay here," Morwen said to Chaos. "It's possible that Telemain will be bouncing us around with his transport spells, and he's not used to dealing with a crowd. I'd worry about someone getting left behind."

"I'm staying," Jasmine announced with an enormous yawn. "Telemain's spells give me motion sickness."

"*Moving* gives you motion sickness," Trouble muttered. "But the rest of us—"

"Several of you should stay here in case the wizards show up while I'm gone," Morwen pointed out.

"I'll be ready for them." Fiddlesticks jumped onto the window ledge, where he balanced precariously, trying to look fierce and watchful without stepping on Jasmine. "I won't let them in, even if they offer me some fish!"

"You are an example to us all," Miss Eliza said. It was impossible to tell from her tone whether or not she meant it to be sarcastic.

"He'll do better than Jasmine would," Murgatroyd said. "She didn't hear a thing when the mirror went off a bit ago."

Morwen frowned. "Someone called while I was out? Why didn't you mention it?"

"It was that fellow you don't like," Trouble said. "The one with the long name that you won't turn into a toad."

"Arona Michaelear Grinogion Vamist?" Morwen said incredulously.

"That's him. He was annoyed when he didn't see anyone but us." Trouble's tail whipped sideways, up, and then down onto the ground with a thump that showed what he thought of such lack of taste.

" 'Us'? How many of you were in my study when he called?"

Several of the cats shifted uncomfortably and looked away.

"Oh, never mind," Morwen said. "Vamist will have to wait; I haven't time for him now. The fate of the Enchanted Forest is much more important than his idiotic notions."

"She sounds cranky," Fiddlesticks said to Jasmine. "Do you think she'll turn him into a toad after all?"

Before anyone could answer, there was a loud *thwump* from the other side of the house. Fiddlesticks fell off the window ledge, and all of the rest of the cats except Jasmine jumped. The moment he landed, Trouble leapt for the back door with an angry growl, Chaos and Murgatroyd close behind.

"Wait for me!" Fiddlesticks yelled, scrambling to his feet. "Wait—"

"Morwen!" The shout came from the front yard as Morwen rose unhurriedly to her feet.

"That sounds like Kazul," Scorn said.

"I suspect it is," Morwen said. "Come along, Scorn. It's time to leave."

9

In Which the Expedition Leaves the Enchanted Forest at Last

The rest of the cats, even Jasmine, followed Morwen and Scorn through the house and out onto the front porch. Kazul was standing in the center of the yard, along with Telemain and Killer. The donkey was still floating a good six inches above the ground, and he looked extremely uncomfortable. Standing beside him was Mendanbar, who was frowning ferociously, and Cimorene, who seemed to be trying to suppress a satisfied smile. With some dismay, Morwen noted that Cimorene now had a small pack slung over one shoulder and a slim sword belted to her waist.

The cats flowed across the yard and converged on Kazul. Making little noises of satisfaction, all nine of the cats scrambled up the dragon's sides. Their claws rasped against Kazul's scales, making Cimorene wince, but neither they nor the dragon seemed to notice.

Morwen looked at Telemain while the cats draped themselves contentedly all over Kazul. "I thought you were going to explain to him why he couldn't come along," she said, nodding sideways at Mendanbar.

"I did," Telemain said grumpily.

"Then what is he doing here?"

"Making trouble?" Scorn suggested from a comfortable perch on Kazul's left shoulder.

"He'd better not be," Trouble said. "That's my job." He stretched himself full length along the lower part of Kazul's neck, beside her spinal ridges, his tail and one front paw dangling lazily.

"I'm taking you to the edge of the Enchanted Forest," Mendanbar said. "I can do that much, at least, even if I can't come with you. My magic will get you there faster than anything else, and you'll be safe from most of the things that live in the forest if you're with me."

"I see." That explained Telemain's bad mood: he hated having to admit that anyone's magic was better than his, even the King's. Morwen looked at Cimorene. "What about you?"

"I'm coming with you," Cimorene said. Mendanbar scowled fiercely as if he wanted to object, but before he could, Cimorene hurried on, "I *have* to. Otherwise you'll have as much difficulty with the sword as I hope those blasted wizards are having right now."

Kazul snorted angrily, sending out a large ball of smoke, which made everyone in front of her cough. "If they aren't having trouble now, they will soon."

Morwen gave Kazul a stern look over the tops of her glasses. "We are going on this expedition to recover Mendanbar's sword, Kazul. We aren't trying to destroy the entire Society of Wizards."

"Yet," said Trouble.

"You be quiet, or I'll leave you at home," Morwen said. "Now, would someone explain to me just *why* Cimorene has to come along?"

"Resonance and half-hard deflection mechanisms," Telemain said. "Which are—"

"—as clear as mud," Kazul put in.

Telemain looked annoyed. "I wasn't talking to you. Morwen understands what I mean."

"Most of the time," Morwen said.

"I think he means that Mendanbar's sword is painful to touch, unless you happen to belong to the King's family," Cimorene said. "And the longer it stays outside the forest, the harder it is to handle."

"The deflection increases exponentially," Telemain said. "Rather like the magic leakage we discussed earlier, only the defense spells won't slow down the deflection. By this time, it is undoubtedly past the transfer-resonance point."

"So the Society of Wizards can't use the sword against us." Morwen smiled grimly. "Good. I'd been wondering about that."

"Unfortunately, *you* can't use it, either," Cimorene said. "If Telemain is right about the timing—"

"And I am."

"—then in a day or two nobody but a member of the Royal Family will be able to pick up the sword at all, much less carry it back to the Enchanted Forest. So since Mendanbar and I are the only members of the

Royal Family right now, and since Mendanbar has to stay in the forest—"

"—you *have* to come with us to retrieve the sword," Morwen finished, raising an eyebrow. "I see."

Cimorene grinned. "Telemain explained it at least three times at the castle, and by the time he and Mendanbar finished arguing, I had a pretty good idea what he meant, even if he never did say it straight out."

"I did, too!" Telemain said indignantly. "Several times."

"Not so I understood."

"That is unfortunately not very surprising," Morwen said. "Mendanbar, your sword is very inconveniently designed."

"Don't blame *me,*" Mendanbar said. "The blasted thing came with the kingdom."

"Hmph." Morwen glanced around. "What about Killer? Why is he here?"

Killer's ears twitched anxiously forward. "They told me I was supposed to come. Is it all right?"

"Once we're away from the interference patterns of the Enchanted Forest, we should be able to trace the residual energy in the morphological field trap," Telemain said. "At that point, a standard locus delimiter should —"

"Telemain," Kazul said in a warning tone.

Morwen rolled her eyes. "He thinks we can use what's left of the size-changing spell on Killer to find the wizards. But are you sure there's enough, Telemain?"

"I can't tell until we're out of the forest," Telemain said. "The interference—" He glanced at Kazul and stopped.

"I understand," Morwen said. "But remember: bringing him along was your idea, so you're responsible for keeping him out of trouble."

"And he'd better do a good job," Trouble said. "If that overgrown blue idiot steps on *my* tail, he'll wish he'd never left his rabbit hole."

"I *already* wish I'd never left my hole," Killer said. "Rabbits aren't supposed to have adventures. Our temperaments aren't suited to them."

"Are you people going to stand around talking all day?" Kazul asked pointedly. "Or are we going wizard hunting?"

"*Sword* hunting, Kazul, if you please," Morwen said. "And I am ready to leave as soon as we decide which way we're heading."

There was a pause while Cimorene, Telemain, and Mendanbar looked at each other. Scorn snickered. "Look at them! They didn't even think of that."

"The central office of the Society of Wizards is in the Brown Forest," Telemain said at last. "We should probably start there."

"Why waste time?" Kazul said. "The wizards wouldn't be stupid enough to take Mendanbar's sword to their main office."

"Antorell would," Cimorene said.

"Where is the Brown Forest?" Killer asked timidly. "It doesn't sound very . . . appetizing."

"It's worse than it sounds," Telemain told him. "The Brown Forest is actually a corner of the Great Southern Desert."

Frowning, Cimorene looked at Telemain. "I always thought the Brown Forest was a dead woods. Are you sure it's really a desert?"

Telemain nodded. "I've been there."

"You have?" Kazul said. "Why?"

"I wanted to learn wizardry, and the school the Society of Wizards runs is the only—"

"You wanted to be a *wizard?*" Kazul said, outraged.

"No," Telemain said in the too-patient tone of someone who has had to give the same explanation far too many times. "I didn't want to *be* a wizard. I wanted to *study* them. Their magical methods are unique, and magicians have been attempting to figure them out for a long, long time."

"And you thought they would tell you if you asked politely?" Cimorene said.

Telemain shrugged. "It was worth a try. Anyway, I've been to the Brown Forest in the Great Southern Desert. I can probably even find the area where the central office of the Society of Wizards was when I was there."

"The area where it *was?*" Kazul said.

"They move the building every couple of months," Telemain explained. "I don't know whether they do it to stay hard to find or whether they take turns practicing the relocation spell."

"No wonder they keep trying to steal other people's magic," Kazul muttered. "They waste what they've got moving buildings around."

"South, then?" Mendanbar said, glancing around. "Very well." He raised a hand, then paused. "Morwen, are you taking *all* your cats along on this expedition?"

"Phooey," said Murgatroyd. "I was hoping no one would think of that."

"Just Trouble and Scorn," Morwen said, giving the

cats a stern look. "The rest of you should get down now."

Cats flowed along Kazul's back and off her shoulders, until only Trouble and Scorn remained. When the whole crowd had reached the porch, Morwen nodded to Mendanbar. An instant later, gray mist rose, thickened to hide the house and forest, then faded to reveal a grove of slender young trees, none of which were much taller than Kazul. They looked odd and spindly, and it was a moment before Morwen realized that they only seemed scraggly by comparison to the giant oaks that surrounded her house.

"This is as far as I can take you," Mendanbar said unhappily. "The edge of the Enchanted Forest is over there."

"What about getting back in, once we leave?" Telemain asked.

"If we recover the sword, getting into the forest won't be a problem," Cimorene said. "If we don't—"

"I'll keep an eye on the border," Mendanbar said. "As soon as I see you, I'll come out to meet you."

"Don't worry about watching for us," Morwen said. "Worry about the wizards. We'll call on the magic mirror when we're ready to come back."

"And a couple of times before then, just to say hi," Cimorene put in.

Mendanbar looked at Cimorene for a long minute, then turned to Telemain. "Are you *sure* I can't leave the Enchanted Forest?"

"Not without destroying the energy loop that prevents the Society of Wizards from primary absorption inside the forest," Telemain said.

"Then can't you transfer the spell's focus from me to Cimorene?"

"Hey!" said Cimorene, frowning. "Who says I want to be a focus?"

"No," Telemain said to Mendanbar. "The top links connect directly to the central—"

" 'No' is quite enough," Morwen said. "Didn't you go over all this at the castle?"

"Yes," Cimorene said. "Mendanbar is just trying to keep me out of this." She stepped forward and drew Mendanbar a little away from the others. "Look, dear, there's nothing you can . . ." Her voice faded to a murmur.

"How far is the Brown Forest from here?" Morwen asked Telemain.

"Three transports and a two-day walk." Telemain looked at Kazul and frowned suddenly. His gaze traveled down the dragon's neck, across her wings and massive back, and out along her tail. "Make that five transports and a two-day walk. I didn't have quite so much to move last time."

"I could stay here," Killer offered hopefully.

"No, you couldn't," Morwen said. "Telemain needs you to find the wizards. Why a two-day walk, Telemain?"

"Because the Society of Wizards has established an interference pattern around the Brown Forest."

"So?" said Scorn.

"So that means it isn't safe to use transportation spells anywhere near the forest," Morwen said.

"I bet you could break it," Trouble said. "Wizards are wimps."

"Maybe," Morwen said. "And maybe you would end up with Killer's ears and Scorn's tail. Even simple interference patterns are tricky, and this one has the whole Society of Wizards behind it."

"Committees never do a good job," Scorn said, but she did not pursue the issue.

"Are you sure you need the donkey?" Kazul asked. "Because I think I can carry everyone else for at least a little way, and that would cut down on the travel time."

Killer's ears pricked up, then drooped as Telemain shook his head. "Without Killer we'd have to hunt for the Society of Wizards' building. We'd probably lose more time than we gained."

Kazul shook her head irritably. "Well, if you human people didn't waste so much time arguing, we'd —oh, good, Cimorene's finished."

Turning, Morwen saw Mendanbar and Cimorene coming toward them. Mendanbar's expression was even more unhappy than before, and Cimorene looked equally sober. "Ready to go?" she asked as they reached the group.

"Whenever you are," Telemain replied.

"Cimorene . . . ," said Mendanbar.

"Don't start," Cimorene said in a gentle tone. "One of us has to go, and you can't."

"If Telemain and Morwen weren't with you, I'd say let the wizards have the blasted sword," Mendanbar muttered. "It isn't worth the risk."

"Telemain and Morwen?" Kazul muttered. "What am I, diced troll food?"

Cimorene kissed Mendanbar's nose. "You'd say 'let the wizards have the sword,' but you wouldn't mean it. Don't worry, I'll be all right." She turned to Morwen, her eyes suspiciously bright. "Come on, let's go before he thinks of another objection."

Morwen nodded and started off. The edge of the Enchanted Forest was only a few yards away, clearly visible as a sharp line where the bright green moss stopped and ordinary grass began. At the border, Morwen waited a moment for everyone to line up, then they all crossed at more or less the same time. Telemain had them walk several yards, to get away from the "field influences," before he was satisfied that his transportation spell would work properly. Then, frowning in concentration, he made a circling gesture and muttered under his breath. The trees melted and shifted, then solidified into an open field.

"One down, four to go," said Telemain.

10

In Which Telemain Works Very Hard

Telemain had to stop and rest for a while after the second transportation spell, and after the third he looked so pale that Morwen said, "We don't *have* to go on immediately, you know. We've got at least one more day, and probably two, before the sword reaches the critical point."

"It *is* getting late." Telemain puffed as if he had been running hard for a long time. "Still, I'm quite capable of casting another spell or two."

Cimorene glanced at the tall pines that surrounded them and dug an experimental toe into the spongy accumulation of needles underfoot. "If you're sure it won't be too much—"

"We're going to have to spend the night somewhere, and this looks like as good a place as any," Morwen broke in quickly. "Better than some."

"Boring," said Trouble. "It looks boring. Jasmine would love it. Let's try for somewhere more interesting."

Kazul coiled her tail loosely around the base of one of the trees and stretched herself out on the ground. "It's comfortable, and there's plenty of room."

"I thought you were in a hurry," Telemain said irritably. "Do you want to find Mendanbar's sword or not?"

"If you wear yourself out doing transports, you won't be able to do the locating spell," Morwen said as Cimorene opened her mouth to speak.

"I'm not worn out!"

Cimorene closed her mouth and gave Telemain a long, thoughtful look.

Good, thought Morwen. *Now if I can just get Telemain to agree to stop transporting before he falls over . . .* "If we go on, where will we land next?"

"I'm not sure," Telemain admitted. "Normally, I transfer from here straight to the edge of the Great Southern Desert, but the interval is incompatible with the number of people and the mass I'm transporting on this occasion. Given the ratios, I would approximate a landing site at three-fifths of the normal distance."

"Do you know what we'd find there?" Morwen asked, ignoring Cimorene's puzzled expression.

"No."

"Then we're better off here," Morwen said in a tone intended to discourage further discussion. "It looks comfortable and quiet, and the next stop might not be either." She stepped closer to Telemain and murmured, "And we should be careful not to let Cimorene get too tired."

"Oh!" Telemain sighed in relief. "Of course. Very well, we'll camp here, and go on in the morning."

Cimorene glanced at Morwen suspiciously, but all she said was, "That's settled, then. Why don't you rest for a few minutes while we set things up?"

Killer's nose twitched. "Does that mean we'll get dinner soon? Because I'm hungry."

"Again? All those layers of spells must be affecting your metabolism," Morwen said. "Or didn't Cimorene's cook feed you properly before you left the castle?"

"Oh, he had plenty to eat," Scorn said. "He was gorging himself when we left, and he had nearly half an hour after that before Telemain brought him and the others to the house. You should have seen him, Morwen. He's worse than Fiddlesticks with a plate of fish."

"It's not my fault," Killer said in a plaintive tone. "I can't help being hungry. I just *am*."

"Well, we can't get anything for you to eat until after we've set up camp," Morwen said. "Telemain, is there a source of water around anywhere?"

Telemain directed her to a small pool a short distance away. As Morwen set off, Cimorene fell into step beside her. Once they were too far from the others for anyone to hear, Cimorene said, "I'm sorry I wasn't more help with Telemain, Morwen. I was so worried about Mendanbar's sword that I didn't see how tired he was until he snapped at you. How did you convince him to stay here?"

"I told him you needed to rest."

"You told him *I* needed to—Morwen! I'm not sick. I'm going to have a baby, that's all. I feel *fine*." Cimorene hesitated. "Well, mostly. Sometimes in the mornings my stomach gets a little queasy. But that's not the point."

"No. The point is that *Telemain* needs rest." Morwen pushed aside a low-hanging branch and looked at Cimorene. "Do you really want an overtired magician transporting you? I let someone do that. Once."

"What happened?"

"I ended up forty leagues west of where I wanted to be, and I had an upset stomach for a week afterward. No one had a spare broomstick, so I had to fly home on a borrowed rake. All forty leagues. In the rain. It's the only time in my life I've been airsick."

Cimorene shuddered. "I can see why you'd want to keep Telemain from overextending himself. I just wish you'd thought of some other way to do it."

Pushing through a sweep of long, prickly pine branches, they found the pool Telemain had described. Morwen pulled the collapsible bucket out of her sleeve and filled it, and they started back to the others.

Just before they reached the camp, Cimorene paused. "Morwen, how tired *is* Telemain?"

"He could probably do one more transport without any problems," Morwen admitted. "Two more are definitely out of the question. And if we land in the middle of a battle or on top of a troll's hill—"

"I see."

Morwen nodded. "I prefer not to take chances."

"But a smaller spell wouldn't be a problem for him, would it?"

"What did you have in mind?"

Cimorene blushed slightly. "Well, I did promise I'd call Mendanbar whenever I could. And even if I'd had room for a full-sized magic mirror in my pack, I wouldn't have brought one because they're too breakable. I was hoping Telemain . . ."

"I understand." Morwen thought for a minute. "The hardest part of Telemain's magic-mirror spell is making it permanent. He shouldn't have any difficulty with a temporary speaking spell, especially if he has a chance to rest first. Ask him about it after dinner."

"I will," Cimorene said with a smile.

Cimorene's cook had provided plenty of food for the people and cats, so dinner for them was fairly straightforward. After some initial grumbling, Killer nibbled at low-hanging pine branches and even admitted that they didn't taste too bad, once he got used to them. Since there was not enough of anything to make a dragon-sized meal, Kazul left to forage for herself.

As soon as she finished eating, Cimorene broached the subject of the speaking spell with Telemain. The magician frowned and patted his pockets.

"I believe I have the necessary materials," he said. "All I need is an object."

Waving at her pack, the various cups and containers Morwen had produced from her sleeves, and the half-empty water bucket, Cimorene said, "Aren't there plenty of things around?"

"No, I mean an object for the *enchantment*. Something with the correct reflective properties. To be compatible with the existing enchantment on the castle mirror, a provisional communications spell must employ the same similarities and reversals of congruence as the original. Therefore—"

"You need a mirror, right?" Cimorene guessed.

"No," Morwen said. "He needs something *like* a mirror. Something you can see your reflection in."

"Maybe if we polish the dishes?" Cimorene said, eyeing the dented metal dubiously.

The castle cook had sent along four of the oldest tin plates Morwen had ever seen. They were suitable for camping, but not, Morwen thought, for spell making.

"What about this?" Scorn said, circling the water bucket.

"Yes, that might do." Hastily, Morwen picked up the bucket, barely in time to keep Trouble from setting his paws on the rim to peer in and collapsing it. "What do you think, Telemain?"

"Between the metallic surfaces and the water, the reflective properties appear to be adequate," Telemain said after a moment's inspection. "As long as there is no previous enchantment, it should do."

"Does carrying it in my sleeve count?"

"Since the bucket is no longer inside the spell's sphere of influence, it should have no impact on the application of a transitory enchantment."

"What does he mean?" Killer asked.

"It doesn't count—as long as the bucket isn't in my sleeve when he tries to enchant it," Morwen said. "How long will the spell last, Telemain?"

"About a quarter of an hour." Telemain set the bucket in front of him and began removing things from his pockets. "It should return to its base state by dawn tomorrow."

Setting up the speaking spell did not take long. Morwen watched Telemain closely as he crouched over the bucket, for he still seemed unusually tired, but he had no difficulty in casting the enchantment.

"There," he said finally, sitting back on his heels. "You can go ahead now, Cimorene. Just don't move the bucket."

"All right, then," Cimorene said, though she looked as if she felt a little silly.

"Mirror, mirror, on the wall,
I would like to make a call."

The water in the bucket turned white. "Tell it who to find," Morwen said softly.

"I wish to speak to Mendanbar, the King of the Enchanted Forest," Cimorene said.

With a swish and a gurgling noise, the milky color cleared. "Who's there?" snarled the wooden gargoyle. "Nobody's home and they can't be bothered, so—oh, hello, Your Majesty."

"Hello. *Is* Mendanbar at home?" said Cimorene.

"Sure. Hey, King! There's somebody on the mirror you should talk to!" the gargoyle shouted.

"Tell him who it is," Cimorene commanded.

"Aw, you spoil all my fun," grumbled the gargoyle, but it yelled, "It's Queen Cimorene!"

An instant later, the picture in the water shifted rapidly, then steadied to show King Mendanbar. "Cimorene! Is everything all right?"

"Everything's fine," Cimorene said. "We're halfway to the Great Southern Desert—"

"About three-fifths of the way, actually," said Telemain.

"—and we decided to stop for the night. How are things at home?"

"I caught a couple of wizards prowling around the forest right after you left," Mendanbar said. "You can tell Telemain that his wizard-melting spell works just fine."

"Kazul will be disappointed," Cimorene said. "We haven't seen any traces of wizards, and I think she's been hoping for a good fight."

"Well, tell her to be careful if you do run across them," Mendanbar said. "One of the ones I melted was carrying dragonsbane."

"Oh, dear. Maybe I should send Kazul home."

"You can try."

They both paused. In the brief silence, Morwen caught Telemain's eye and nodded toward the far side of the clearing. Telemain looked puzzled, then suddenly his expression changed and he rose hastily and joined her.

"We might as well give them a few moments' privacy," said Morwen when they were out of earshot. "Unless you have to stay nearby to maintain the mirror spell?"

"No, the spell is self-maintaining once it's established," Telemain said. "If someone wants to make another call, I'll have to reset everything, but she and Mendanbar can talk as long as they like without worrying about any sudden termination."

Trouble appeared around the trunk of a pine and leaned against it, scratching his back against the bark.

"Well, I hope they don't go on much longer. You wouldn't *believe* how mushy they're getting."

"I don't want to hear about it," Morwen said.

"What's that?" Telemain asked. "Is something wrong?"

"Only a cat's usual refusal to let morals interfere with satisfying his curiosity," Morwen said. "Don't ask. It only encourages him."

Fortunately, Cimorene and Mendanbar did not chat for very much longer. Later, when Cimorene reported the conversation to Kazul, the dragon refused to consider leaving.

"I want some wizards, and one way or another I am going to get them," Kazul said. "If I don't go on to the central office of the Society of Wizards, I'll go back to the Enchanted Forest and hunt up a few of them there, dragonsbane or no dragonsbane."

"I don't think that's necessary," Cimorene said quickly. "Mendanbar seems to have everything under control."

"For now," said Scorn.

Not for the first time, Morwen was glad that Cimorene and Telemain, at least, could not understand what her cats were saying.

11

In Which They Make an Unexpected Detour

The next morning, much to Morwen's relief, Telemain appeared to have recovered: Without tiring, he walked briskly to and from the stream to wash up, and his color was nearly normal. After breakfast, he arranged everyone to his satisfaction and muttered the transportation spell.

They materialized on a sunny, grass-covered hillside, and as soon as their feet were firmly planted, Telemain sat down.

"Telemain?" Morwen said with concern. The magician looked a little gray.

"I'm all right," Telemain said. "I just need a minute to catch my breath."

Killer's long blue ears pricked up. "How long a minute? Have I got time for a snack? Because I think I smell a patch of clover off to the left there, and I'm hungry."

"I don't know what you're complaining about," Kazul said. "*You* had plenty of breakfast. Four cheese sandwiches aren't much of a meal for a dragon."

"Five," said Trouble.

"Pine needles are not very filling," Killer said with dignity. "Besides, I want to see what the clover is like outside the Enchanted Forest. I may not get the chance again."

Flicking a look at Telemain, Morwen said, "Go ahead, Killer. Just don't get out of sight."

Killer ambled off, his hooves just grazing the tips of the waving grasses. "What a good thing you got him stabilized," Morwen said to Telemain. "Otherwise he'd be walking around Kazul's head by now."

"It would serve him right," Scorn said, switching her tail. "That idiot rabbit is worse than Fiddlesticks."

"Nobody's worse than Fiddlesticks," said Trouble.

Scorn gave him a green glare, then bounded over to Kazul. Two seconds later, both cats were perched on the dragon's back, basking in the sun. Smiling slightly, Morwen found a sun-warmed rock and sat down. Cimorene joined her at once, and though Telemain gave them both a suspicious frown, he did not comment.

"It's so nice to be able to just sit down, without worrying about what you're sitting on," Cimorene said. "In the Enchanted Forest, you have to be careful that you don't land on someone who's been transformed into a flower or a rock."

"Or sit on something that will transform *you* into a flower or a rock," Telemain added. He appeared to have his breath back, but he still looked a little pale, so Morwen did not suggest that they continue.

The drowsy silence was broken by an earsplitting bray. "Eee-augh! Go away!" yelled Killer. "Morwen said I could eat this, and I'm going to. Leave me alone!"

Morwen looked up. The curve of the hill hid the donkey from sight, along with whatever he was shouting at.

"Blast that creature," Morwen muttered, getting to her feet. "I told him to stay in sight. No, you stay here, Telemain," she added as the magician started to follow. "There's no need to let him inconvenience both of us."

Nodding, Telemain settled back.

He must really be tired, or he'd disagree, Morwen thought. *Perhaps I can get Kazul or Cimorene to override his objections to staying here, or—no, it will be better if Trouble gets conveniently lost for a few hours. I'll have to speak to him as soon as I'm done with Killer.*

As she came around the hill, she saw a tall, gray-haired man in baggy blue overalls with a length of rope in one hand and an empty bucket in the other. Standing at the far edge of the clover patch, he stared expressionlessly at Killer and Morwen.

"This your donkey, ma'am?" the man asked.

"Not exactly," Morwen said. "What seems to be the problem?"

"He says I can't eat any more," Killer complained. "And I'd only just figured out how to get at it, too."

Morwen glanced down. Below Killer's front hooves, a double handspan of grass and clover had been trimmed several inches below the surrounding meadow. "So I see. How did you manage it?"

"Well, if I kneel down and stretch way out—"

"Excuse me, ma'am," said the man in the overalls, setting his bucket at his feet, "but if this ain't your donkey, whose is it?"

"He doesn't belong to anyone in particular," Morwen said. "And he's not actually a donkey. Why?"

The man in the overalls, who had begun uncoiling the length of rope, paused. "Not a donkey, eh?" He studied Killer intently for a moment. "Blue *is* kind of an unusual color for a donkey."

"What's he getting at, Morwen?" Killer's ears waggled nervously.

"Quiet, Killer," Morwen said.

"And I got to admit that donkeys don't normally talk much," the man added. "So what is he? Enchanted prince? Knight? Circus sideshow performer?"

"Rabbit," Morwen said. "Judging from his behavior, a permanently hungry rabbit."

"Huh." The man in the overalls eyed Killer speculatively. "A rabbit named Killer. Amazing, the things people come up with. How'd he end up a blue donkey?"

"It's a long story," Morwen said. "Killer, why don't you go back to the others?"

"But what about the clover? I was just getting started. And it *is* different—not so crunchy, and not as sweet, and there's sort of a cinnamon undertaste that—"

"Not now, Killer. Go let the others know what's happening."

"Oh, all right." Muttering sullenly, Killer started back around the hill.

"What's this about others?" demanded the man in

the overalls as Morwen turned back to him. "How many of you are there?"

"Seven, altogether," Morwen said.

"There are *seven* of you trampling across my fields and ruining the harvest?" the farmer asked, plainly appalled.

"Not exactly. Killer couldn't trample anything right now if he tried, and the rest of us haven't moved around much."

The farmer shook his head. "It was bad enough having that donkey or rabbit or whatever eating up my crops, but this! I want the lot of you out, right now."

"Crops?" Morwen looked pointedly to the left, then to the right, then raised her chin and stared directly at the man in the overalls. "Grass and clover?"

"Hay," the man said, unperturbed.

"Hey what?" said Cimorene's voice. "Morwen, who is this and what is going on? Killer said something about trespassers, but then he got into an argument with your cats, and it's a little hard to follow when you can't understand half of the conversation."

"This appears to be the man who owns this hill," Morwen said.

"Name of MacDonald, ma'am," the man said, nodding politely. "And this is my farm, and I'd appreciate it if you'd take your friend and your donkey and your cats elsewhere."

"I'm Cimorene, the Queen of the Enchanted Forest," Cimorene said. "Pleased to meet you, Farmer MacDonald. And we'll be leaving just as soon as our magician recovers a bit more. I'm sorry if we've caused a problem."

"Queen, eh?" MacDonald's eyes narrowed speculatively. "Little unusual to find a queen out adventuring. Mostly it's princes and younger sons, and once in a while a princess."

"So I'm unusual," Cimorene said.

"I wasn't criticizing," MacDonald said peaceably. "I just wondered if you'd be in the market for some vegetables."

"Vegetables? Why would I—"

"I got a full line of specialty crops," the farmer went on. "My peas are perfectly round, and hard as rock. I sell 'em by the bag if you want to scatter them on the floor for maidens disguised as huntsmen to walk on, or you can buy one at a time for sticking under the mattress of a visiting princess."

"I don't think I—"

"Then there's straw, first quality, for spinning into gold. I can deliver as much as you want, on a regular schedule. I grow four kinds of grain—oats, barley, millet, and wheat—on the same plants, so it's harvested premixed. I sell it by the bushel, to people who want to test someone by making them sort out the different kinds. And beans, naturally. I got the kind that jump and the kind that grow giant stalks. I've got apples, poisoned or gold, in several varieties; extra-large pumpkins for turning into coaches; and walnuts with anything you want inside, from a miniature dog to a dress as shining as the stars."

"I appreciate the offer," Cimorene said, "but I don't think I need any of those things."

"You wouldn't happen to have any invisible dusk-blooming chokevines, would you?" Morwen asked.

"No, I don't grow ornamentals," MacDonald replied. "I stick to vegetables, fruit, and nuts. Farm things. I'm hoping to branch out into livestock soon."

Cimorene blinked. "What sort of livestock?"

"Oh, little dogs that laugh, winged horses, geese that lay golden eggs, that sort of thing. That's why I'm growing hay." The farmer waved at the hillside. "I want to have it on hand when the horses arrive."

"It's not enchanted hay, is it?" Morwen asked with sudden misgiving.

"Not exactly. Why?"

"Killer tends to react . . . oddly when he's exposed to new enchantments." Nothing seemed to have happened yet, though. At least, Morwen hadn't heard any horrified braying since Killer disappeared over the hill. Perhaps it would be all right.

MacDonald shrugged. "I use enchanted fertilizer to help it grow, but the hay itself is nothing special. Winged horses eat pretty much the same thing as regular horses, plus a little birdseed."

"You sound as if you've thought about it quite a bit," Cimorene said.

"Had to," MacDonald said, nodding. "This farm's been in the family for a long time, but I couldn't make a living running it the way my dad did. Here a horse, there a pig—that just doesn't work anymore. These days, you have to have a plan. So I decided to specialize. Sure you don't need anything?"

"Not right now," Cimorene said, "but I'll keep you in mind."

"Thanks." The farmer hesitated. "About that blue donkey—"

"He isn't a donkey," Morwen reminded him. "He's an enchanted rabbit."

"Oh, that's right. Pity. He'd make an interesting start at stocking the barnyard." Fingering his rope thoughtfully, MacDonald stared off in the direction Killer had taken.

"I don't think you'd want him," Cimorene said. "He doesn't seem to be good for much."

"And he eats a great deal," Morwen added. "Most of it unsuitable, inconvenient, or both. Besides, it's time we were leaving."

"What about my hay?"

Morwen glanced at the nibbled clover and raised an eyebrow. "Killer hardly touched it. In a couple of days, you won't be able to tell which part of the patch he got at."

"Well . . ."

"Then that's settled," Cimorene said in a tone that somehow reminded everyone that this was the Queen of the Enchanted Forest talking, and if she said it was settled, it had better *be* settled. "It's been nice meeting you, Mr. MacDonald, and I shall certainly mention your special crops to my friends. Now, we really must be going." She turned and swept off.

Nodding a brisk farewell to MacDonald, Morwen followed. Halfway around the hill, she glanced back and saw MacDonald frowning uncertainly after them. *At least he isn't chasing after us,* she thought. *Goodness knows how he'd react if he saw Kazul.*

The same thought had apparently occurred to Cimorene. "We need to leave right away, if we can," she said as soon as they reached the others. "Can you manage it, Telemain?"

"Of course," the magician said. "But what's the problem?"

"Nothing dangerous, but if we stay we're likely to waste the whole afternoon arguing. I'll explain later."

"Wait a minute," Morwen said as Telemain climbed to his feet. "Where's Scorn?"

"She went after you," Trouble said.

"Bother," said Morwen. "I'm sorry, Cimorene, but—"

An arrow path of grass stirred and shifted. An instant later, Scorn leapt for Morwen's back. Her claws dug into the folds of material, and with another brief effort she pulled herself the rest of the way up to Morwen's shoulder, where she perched, purring smugly.

"No wonder you wear loose robes," Cimorene said.

Balancing carefully, Scorn stretched. Then the purring stopped and she said, "That farmer is coming after you, Morwen. I thought you'd want to know."

"Scorn says MacDonald is on his way," Morwen said to the rest of them. "If you really want to avoid him, Cimorene, we should go now."

"Then let's *go*." Cimorene looked at Telemain.

"Everyone here? Very well, then." Eyes narrowed in unwonted concentration, Telemain raised his hands and recited the spell.

The hillside wavered like a reflection in a suddenly disturbed pool. Reluctantly, it began to melt and shift. Morwen caught a glimpse of MacDonald's face, too distorted to tell whether his expression was one of astonishment or fear, before the scene became unrecognizable.

Suddenly, everything froze. For an impossibly long instant, they hung between greenish blurs and brown blobs. Then, with a painful jerk, everything darkened and slammed into proper shapes once more. Morwen dropped two inches into a puddle of mud. The landing jarred her glasses loose and tore Scorn from her shoulder. Morwen managed to catch the cat, but her glasses vanished into the mud. Behind them, there was a squishy *thwump* as Kazul landed, followed by a yowl from Trouble and various startled noises from Killer and Cimorene.

"Drat," Morwen muttered, swallowing hard. "I knew I should have brought a stomach remedy." The air was damp and smelled like rotten eggs, which didn't help any.

"And boots," Scorn said, relaxing in Morwen's hands.

"Definitely boots," Morwen agreed. The mud was cold, soft, and ankle deep, and between the gloom and her missing glasses she could not spot a better place to step to. Assuming, of course, that there *was* a better place to stand.

"Morwen?" Cimorene called. "Where are you?"

"Where are *we*, is the question," Scorn said.

"Quiet," said Morwen. "Over here, Cimorene. Scorn, I'm going to hunt for my glasses, and I'll need both hands. If you don't want to walk around in this, you'd better climb up on my back."

With a disdainful snort, Scorn scrambled out of Morwen's grasp and back to her shoulder. Slowly, Morwen bent forward, giving Scorn time to adjust her balance. Holding her sleeves out of the way with one hand, she fished in the mud with the other.

A series of sucking noises and squelches came near. "Morwen, *what* are you doing?" Cimorene asked.

She was muddy to the elbows, and she held her drawn sword in one hand.

"Looking for my glasses," Morwen replied. "Unfortunately, I don't seem to—Wait a minute." Carefully, she worked her hand free of the mud. "There. Now all I have to do is clean them."

"Easier to say than do, in this muck," Cimorene said. "Didn't you bring an extra pair?"

"Chaos broke my extra pair last week." Morwen squinted at the mud-covered glasses, then shrugged. Pinching a fold of material from her robe, she began wiping the lenses. "The replacements haven't been delivered yet."

"Well, I'm afraid I can't help. I slipped when we landed, and even my handkerchiefs are full of mud. Morwen, where *are* we? This doesn't look like the edge of a desert."

"No kidding," said Scorn.

"Ask Telemain," Morwen said, putting on her glasses. "He should have some idea where we were when he lost control." The lenses were still streaky, but at least she could see.

A worry line appeared between Cimorene's eyebrows, below the mud that smeared her forehead. "I don't know where Telemain is," she said. "I was hoping he was over here, with you."

12

Which Is Exceedingly Muddy

Morwen looked around. Here and there, tall, thin trees shot upward from the omnipresent mud. High in the air, they suddenly sprouted a wide, dense mat of twisted branches. Long, fuzzy gray-green strips of moss dangled from the branches, shutting out most of the light, and patches of dirty white fog drifted among the trunks. Between the fog and the shadows, it was hard to be sure of seeing anyone. Even Kazul seemed to melt into the gloom. Only Killer's vivid blue stood out against the muddy colors of the swamp.

"Is everyone else here?" Morwen said. Her stomach was already settling down, which was a relief. The last time this had happened, it had taken much longer.

Cimorene nodded.

"Then I'll look for Telemain. There's bound to be

some residue from the transportation spell for me to trace. The rest of you stay together so I can find you again. If we split up in this mess, we're likely to lose someone permanently."

"I suppose that's best," Cimorene said, but she did not sound happy.

Morwen was not very happy about the arrangement, either, but she did not say anything more as Cimorene squelched back to Kazul. Then, with a resigned sigh, she reached into her left sleeve and pulled out a ball of red yarn and a shiny metal plate three inches across with a small hole near the rim. Focusing her attention on her most recent memories of Telemain's magic, she tied the yarn to the plate. She bent and breathed on the metal, clouding it over, then said quickly,

"Green and growing, show me.
Swift and silent, show me.
Damp and dingy, show me.
Deep and shining, show me what I would see."

With her last words, she released the plate so that it hung free. It spun wildly on the end of the yarn, and she felt it tug lightly to the right, well away from the others. Carefully, she turned, letting the faint pull guide her. It took considerable concentration to follow the spell while slogging through the cold, sticky mud.

"I *thought* something smelled different over this way," Scorn said.

Morwen spared a moment for a glance at the cat. "You might have told me."

"You were busy."

"True. Next time, tell me anyway." The tug was growing stronger. Morwen dodged around a tree trunk and almost stepped on Telemain. He lay face up in the mud, his eyes closed and his skin an unhealthy grayish white. Morwen had to look twice to be sure that he was still breathing.

Stuffing her yarn and the metal plate back into her sleeve, Morwen shouted for Cimorene to come at once and bring the others. Then she crouched next to Telemain to see what she could do for him. Unfortunately, what he needed most was to be warm, dry, and somewhere he could sleep in comfort.

He must have been even more tired than I thought he was, or the backshock wouldn't have affected him this badly, Morwen thought. *He should have said something.*

"Stubborn fool," she said aloud.

"This comes as a surprise?" Scorn said.

"Morwen, what—oh, my." Cimorene squished over as quickly as she could, followed by Killer and Kazul. Trouble, somewhat muddy and damp looking, was clinging with grim determination to a spot high on Kazul's back. The moment the dragon stopped moving, Trouble extended a rear leg and began washing it vigorously. Killer looked unusually pleased with himself, probably because floating six inches off the ground had kept him the only completely dry and unmuddy member of the group.

"What happened?" Kazul asked as Cimorene joined Morwen. "That was *not* one of the most enjoyable experiences I've ever had."

"I'm not completely sure." Morwen reached into her right sleeve and began fishing around. "I'm a witch, not a magician. But I think it's backshock from that transportation spell."

"Backshock?" said Killer.

"If you pull a rubber band too hard, it breaks and snaps your fingers," Cimorene explained. "The same sort of thing can happen when someone loses control of a spell, only it's usually more serious than stinging fingers."

"Oh." Killer looked at Morwen. "Rubber band?"

"Never mind," Morwen said. "Ah, there it is." She pulled her heavy-duty wool camping blanket out of her sleeve, glanced around for a dry spot to put it, and ended by draping it across Killer's back. "Cimorene, we have to get Telemain out of this mud. Help me lift him onto Killer."

"What? Wait a minute!" said Killer, taking two hasty steps backward. "I'm not supposed to do things like this. I'm a *rabbit*."

"You used to be," said Morwen. "Now you're a six-foot floating blue donkey. Hold still."

"But you'll get mud all over me!"

Trouble glanced up from his washing. "Good idea. Can I help?"

"If you do, you'll get muddy, too," Scorn said. She looked at Trouble. "Muddier."

"The mud will get on my blanket," Morwen said. "And I can tell you already that Mendanbar is going to get a really enormous cleaning bill when this is all over."

"But—"

"Don't argue," Kazul said to the donkey. "I'm feeling cross enough already, and my stomach is bothering me."

"The stomachache is a side effect of snapping the transportation spell," Morwen said. "The bad temper is probably from waking up too early. Ready, Cimorene?"

Killer did argue, of course. It took nearly as long to convince him as it took to pry Telemain's unconscious body out of the mud, wrap him in Morwen's blanket, and hoist him onto the donkey's back.

"There," Cimorene panted, steadying Telemain with one hand. "That's done."

"And it looks pretty useless to me," Scorn said. She had joined Trouble on top of Kazul and was watching the whole procedure with an expression of disapproval. "Now that you've got him there, what are you going to do with him?"

Killer shifted his feet in evident unease. "This is really uncomfortable. Isn't there *somewhere* else you could put him?"

"He doesn't care much for riding on you, either," Morwen said. "Don't worry, we'll try to keep it short. Kazul, can you see anything that looks like a way out of here?"

Stretching up to her full height, Kazul peered into the fog. "No. The fog's getting thicker, and the trees all look the same."

"Hey, warn me before you do that," Trouble said reproachfully. "I almost fell off."

Kazul lowered her forelegs and glanced over her shoulder. "That can be arranged."

"It wouldn't matter," Scorn said to Trouble. "All that washing hasn't done much good. You still look like something the dog dragged in."

"You've got wings," Killer said to Kazul. "Why don't you fly up and look around?"

"Because there isn't enough room between these trees for a proper takeoff, because flying in a fog is dangerous, and because I probably couldn't find you again once I got up above the treetops," Kazul said. "The tops of forests all look the same."

"Oh."

"You found Telemain," Cimorene said to Morwen. "Can't you use the same method to find a way out of here?"

"I could if there were any magic left to trace," Morwen said. "Unfortunately, there isn't. Pick a direction."

"That way," said Cimorene, and they started off.

Walking through the swamp was hard work. With every step, the ankle-deep mud sucked at their feet. Twice, Cimorene almost lost one of her short leather boots, and even Kazul had difficulty making headway. The only one who had no problem was Killer. Telemain's added weight did not pull him down at all; his hooves stayed a dry six inches above the muck no matter what. Morwen found herself wondering a little sourly whether the donkey could walk across water the same way he did across the endless mud.

Around noon, Morwen passed out chicken-salad sandwiches to everyone. Her sleeves had protected them from the mud, which was doubly fortunate since Cimorene's pack had leaked and the remains of breakfast were inedible. Unexpectedly, no one complained of a stomachache (though Killer complained about the taste of the lettuce and the bread), and the sandwiches disappeared rapidly.

When they finished eating, they went on. Morwen kept a close but unobtrusive eye on Telemain. Though he did not stir, he did not appear to grow any worse, either, which surprised her a little. She kept both her surprise and her worries to herself.

On and on they waded, until the shadows began to thicken as did the fog. Beads of moisture glistened on Kazul's scales, and the cats complained loudly of the damp. Morwen gave up trying to keep her glasses from clouding over. Telemain remained unconscious, and the worry line between Cimorene's eyebrows grew deeper.

"It'll be dark soon," Cimorene said at last. "We should find somewhere to camp. If there is anywhere. We haven't seen a dry spot since we got here. Killer, where do you think you're going?"

"I'm hungry," Killer said. "If you're going to make me haul people around, the least you could do is let me eat. It's been a long time since lunch."

"There isn't anything *to* eat," Cimorene said.

"Not for you, maybe, but those things over there look edible to me."

"What things?" Feeling slightly annoyed, Morwen took off her glasses and began hunting for a clean patch of robe to wipe them on.

"Those things wrapped around the trees," Killer said, cocking a bright blue ear to his left. "The viney things with the silver leaves. There was one patch of clover back home that had silver leaves sometimes, and it was especially good. Sweet and tart at the same time, and quite strong."

"You're seeing things," Cimorene said. "There aren't any vines on those trees."

"There are, too. You must be looking in the wrong place. Here, I'll show—"

Morwen shoved her glasses back onto her nose and snapped, "Killer, stop right where you are. Don't you take another step toward those vines of yours. If they're really there, they could be very dangerous."

Killer looked at her in disbelief. "They're just *plants*."

"Possibly. Kazul, do you see anything?"

"Trees, fog, and mud," the dragon replied. "Lots and lots of mud. And I agree with Cimorene. We should be trying to find somewhere to camp, not arguing about imaginary vines."

"Not imaginary," Morwen corrected. "Invisible. To be exact, invisible dusk-blooming chokevines." She peered at the trees, wishing she had time to collect one or two of them. Then she shook her head. Cimorene and Kazul were right, and they'd wasted enough time already.

"They don't *look* dangerous," Killer said stubbornly. "And I'm *hungry*."

"The last time you said that, you drank Morwen's wizard-melting water and turned blue," Scorn said.

"Quiet," said Trouble. "Go on, Killer. I would if I were you."

"You hush," said Morwen. "Keep away from those plants, Killer. They're called 'chokevines' for a very good reason. Try to remember you're carrying Telemain, and avoid anything dangerous. And let us know if you see any more of those vines."

"Oh, there are patches of them all over," Killer

said. "We've been walking by them for the last hour. You really can't see them at all? None of you?"

"I can," Trouble said.

Morwen gave him a look. "We'll discuss it later."

As she turned away, a soft globe of light blossomed from the side of one of the trees Killer had pointed out. "What on earth is that?" Cimorene said.

Another light appeared, and another, and suddenly the swamp was full of ghostly radiance. "Invisible dusk-blooming chokevines, all right," Morwen said. "The sun must be setting."

"It's beautiful," Cimorene said. "How long will it last?"

"An hour, maybe two." As she spoke, Morwen moved to Killer's side to check on Telemain's condition once more. His color was no better, and the skin of his wrist was cold and clammy where she touched it to take his pulse. Of course, everything was cold and damp after hours of laboring through the mud. At least his pulse was strong.

"Will he be all right?" Cimorene asked, joining her.

"Probably," Morwen said with more confidence than she felt. The worst case of backshock she had ever seen prior to this trip had regained consciousness in a little over an hour. Telemain had already been out more than twice that long and showed no sign of awakening. Bouncing about on Killer's back should not have delayed his recovery *this* long.

"Look at the bright side," Scorn said. "As long as he's unconscious, he can't go on about things no one else understands."

Realizing that Cimorene and Kazul were watching her anxiously, Morwen shook herself. "What he really needs is warmth, rest, and a bowl of hot broth . . ."

". . . and we aren't going to find them standing here," Cimorene finished for her. "Come on, Killer. We'd better keep moving while we can still see."

In one way, the next half hour of walking was easier than the last couple had been. The invisible dusk-blooming chokevines lit the swamp with a silvery glow, like the light of a hundred miniature moons. As the group went farther along, the vines grew more and more thickly, and their blossoms shone more and more brightly, until even the mud seemed to glisten like liquid silver. Not only was it pretty to look at, but it also made it much easier to see where they were stepping.

After a while, they paused to rest. Morwen checked on Telemain again, with no better results. Frowning, she turned away. If they didn't find somewhere dry and warm soon . . .

"Cimorene, Morwen," said Kazul, "look at these lights."

"I have been, all the time we were walking," Cimorene said. "They're useful as well as pretty."

"No, I mean *look* at them." Kazul stretched out her neck and swiveled her head from one side to the other. "They aren't just growing at random. They're in rows."

Morwen studied the lights. "Not quite. The trees aren't in rows, so the vines can't be, either. But they're close."

"It's as if someone arranged them to light a path," Cimorene said after a moment. "I don't know if I like this."

"I do," Morwen said. "Paths lead somewhere. And

if someone has gone to the trouble of lighting this one up, there's a good chance it leads somewhere useful."

"In that case, why didn't they pave it?"

"Maybe they like mud. Come on, we've only got another hour or so before the lights go out."

With renewed energy, they went on. Less than a quarter of an hour later, they reached a dead end. The invisible dusk-blooming chokevines covered the trees on either side and hung in swirls of glowing silver across the trunks ahead. The only way out was the way they had come.

"Useful, huh?" said Scorn.

"This doesn't make any sense," said Cimorene. "Why would anyone make a path that leads nowhere?" She drew her sword, eyeing the vines doubtfully. "Can we cut our way through, do you think?"

"I don't know," said Kazul, "and I don't care." Her tail thumped into the mud for emphasis, spattering thick, sticky gobs in all directions.

"Uh-oh," said Trouble. "Hang on, Scorn."

The dragon sat back and arched her neck. "I am *not* going to spend another two hours fighting the same mud we just came through. If I must wade through mud, it is at least going to be *new* mud. Get out of my way, the rest of you."

"If you're thinking of diving through the vines, don't," Morwen said, moving sideways. "Invisible dusk-blooming chokevines are very strong, and there are enough of them here to kill even someone as large as you are."

"Not if they've been toasted first." Stretching her head forward until it was only a few yards from the chokevines, Kazul opened her mouth and blew. Long streamers of bright orange fire shot between the trees. Kazul's head moved back and forth, sweeping the flames across the end of the path.

Steam hissed from the mud, and glowing silver blossoms winked out in puffs of ash. As Kazul's flame moved across the tree trunks, it left smaller flickers of fire behind hanging in midair. On the second pass, the flickers spread, outlining leaves and stems in tongues of flame. Blackened spirals slowly materialized around the trees as the fires burned upward and the charred vines lost their invisibility.

"I think that's enough, Kazul," Cimorene said at last.

The fire died. "Good," said the dragon, sounding a little out of breath. "Shall we go on?"

"I think we'd better wait until the mud cools off," Morwen said. "You got a trifle overenthusiastic, I'm afraid."

"No kidding," said Scorn. "Next time, warn us before you do that."

"Killer!" Cimorene shouted. "Come back here!"

"Why?" said the donkey. He stood in the middle of the path Kazul's flame had cleared through the chokevines, flecks of ash drifting through the air around him. Beyond, the fog and darkness closed in once more. "You said it was the vines that were dangerous, and they're gone."

"Even so, we shouldn't split up," Morwen said. "There may be other dangerous things around."

"We haven't seen any so far."

"And that's supposed to mean it's safe?" Scorn shook her head. "Rabbit logic."

"Isn't that a contradiction in terms?" Trouble said.

Morwen sighed. "We may not have seen anything but the chokevines, but that doesn't mean there aren't other dangers."

"All right," Killer said. "But I thought you wanted to get this wizard of yours somewhere dry."

"He's a magician, not a wizard," Morwen said automatically. "And just because Kazul dried out some of the mud—"

"No, no, I'm talking about that tall building in the open space." Killer pointed both ears into the gloom ahead of him and a little to the right. "It looks dry. Why don't we take him there?"

13

In Which They Make a New Acquaintance

Gingerly, Morwen moved forward to take a look at whatever Killer had found. The acrid scent of burned chokevines made her stomach feel queasy again, but the mud turned out to be cool enough to wade through without discomfort. Where Killer stood, it was almost dry enough to be solid ground, and the warmth that remained to filter through her shoes was very welcome.

"Now, where—ah, I see." Dimly visible in the foggy dark, a white tower stood among the trees ahead of them.

"Yes, that looks promising. Let's go." Morwen started forward, and the others followed.

Less than five minutes later, they stood at the foot of the tower. It was at least four stories high, and made of something smooth and pale that did not feel like stone. Ten feet from the base of the tower, the mud changed to hard, bare ground. This gave Morwen and Cimorene a comfortably wide area on which to stand, though Kazul was a little cramped.

"There's no door," Cimorene announced after circling the tower. "No stairs on the outside, either, but there are four windows at the top. One of them is showing a light, so somebody's home."

"But how could anybody get in?" Killer asked.

"Through the windows," Morwen said. "What a pity I didn't bring my broomstick."

"Maybe whoever lives here has some other way of getting inside," Cimorene said.

"There's one way to find out," said Kazul. With Morwen, Cimorene, and Killer in line after her, the dragon edged around the tower until she stood below the single lighted window. Then she sat back and stretched her neck upward, until her head was halfway up the side of the tower.

"Here we go again," said Trouble, wrapping all four paws tightly around one of Kazul's back spines.

"Hello, the tower!" Kazul bellowed. "Who's home? Come out and meet your visitors!"

The window flew open with a force that ought to have shattered the glass. "Go *away!*" shouted someone inside the tower. "She doesn't live here anymore, and if you keep pestering me, I'll burn you to cinders!"

Cimorene's eyes narrowed and she muttered something Morwen could not hear. Then she motioned Morwen and Killer to move back. After a moment's consideration, Morwen stayed where she was. If there were any real danger of being burned, her cats would not still be clinging to Kazul's spikes; their instinct about such things was very good.

"Come out and talk!" Kazul roared again.

A man's head appeared at the window, silhouetted against the light. "I don't want—Good lord, a dragon."

"Don't go away!" Cimorene shouted. "We need to talk to you."

"I wasn't going away," the man yelled down. "Not yet, anyway. What is a dragon doing in the middle of the Smoking Swamp?"

"So that's where we are," Trouble said.

"We missed our way," Morwen called. "And we have an injured companion who needs to rest in a warm, dry place. We were hoping you could help."

"Another one?" The man leaned precariously out, peering into the gloom. "How many of you *are* there?"

"Three humans, a donkey, two cats, and a dragon," Cimorene said. "Are you going to help or not?"

"Help." The man sounded mildly surprised by the idea. "I suppose I could. Since you didn't actually come looking for me."

"What's that got to do with it?" Killer whispered. "I don't understand this person at all."

"I expect we'll find out in a little while," Morwen said. Raising her voice, she called, "Are you going to let us in or not?"

"I think so. Yes, I believe I will. Hold on a minute while I get the laundry basket."

"Basket?" Killer's ears waggled. "I don't like the sound of this."

"Neither do I," said Kazul.

"Don't be unreasonable," Cimorene said to the

dragon. "You can't expect everyone to be able to accommodate a dragon on short notice."

"This place doesn't look as if it could accommodate a dragon on *any* notice," Kazul said.

"Here it comes," said the man's voice above them. "Look out below."

Something large and dark poked out of the window, trembled, and fell. Kazul ducked, and her rear legs slid back into the mud. An instant later, a large straw laundry basket jerked to a stop a foot from the ground, bounced once, and swung twisting in the air. Three short ropes stretched from metal anchors around the basket's rim to a much longer rope that extended upward into the dark.

"One at a time, please," the man called. "And send somebody light first."

"I don't like the sound of that at all," Kazul said.

Morwen studied the laundry basket, nodded, and reached into her left sleeve. "One person at a time? Nonsense. There is no reason to drag things out." She withdrew a fat round jar and opened it. "Trouble, Scorn, I'd like your assistance, please."

Alerted by her tone, the cats slid down Kazul's sides and bounded over. Purring loudly, they took up positions on either side of the laundry basket without further instructions.

"What's that?" Cimorene asked, nodding at the jar Morwen was holding.

"Flying ointment," Morwen said. "It's a standard spell for broomsticks, but it should work equally well on a straw basket. Be quiet for a moment, please."

"What's going on down there? Hurry up, or I'll haul it in without you!"

"Kazul, would you mind?" Morwen flicked a finger at the rope.

"Not at all." Kazul took hold of the knot where all the ropes met, inserting her claws carefully in the gaps between ropes so as not to damage anything.

Satisfied that the laundry basket wasn't going anywhere, Morwen dipped a finger in the flying ointment and smeared it along the basket's rim. The straw soaked it up much faster than a broom handle, so it took longer than she had expected to work her way around the basket. Overhead, the man in the tower shouted again, but Morwen did not bother to listen. Suddenly, as she neared the spot where she had started, Scorn hissed and the laundry basket swayed wildly.

Her concentration broken, Morwen looked up. A palm-sized semicircle had disappeared from the rim of the laundry basket in front of her, and Killer was backing rapidly away. A ragged fringe of straw stuck out around the edges of his mouth.

"Killer!" said Morwen.

"I'm sorry," Cimorene said. "I should have been watching him, but I got too interested in what you were doing."

"Mm hmph *hmphrmph*," said Killer. He swallowed and tried again. "I was *hungry*. You wouldn't let me eat those vine things."

"Straw has no nutritional value," Morwen said. "And after all that's happened to you already, I'd think you'd know better than to take a bite out of something while I'm casting a flying spell on it."

"Oh, I was careful," Killer said. "I aimed for the part you hadn't gotten to yet."

"I think you missed," said Kazul.

Killer's ears pricked up, then dropped. "What? No, I'm sure I—ouch! Oh no, now what? Morwen, this *hurts!*"

"What hurts?"

"My back. Owww! Can't you do something?"

"In a minute," Morwen said. Whatever was happening to Killer, it was unlikely to damage him seriously. Finishing the spell was far more important. To break off now might cause difficulties, and even if it didn't, there wasn't enough of the flying ointment to start over from the beginning.

Morwen turned back to the laundry basket. With two more swipes, she covered the rest of the rim, including the part Killer had bitten out. She wiped her fingers carefully on the side of the laundry basket, nodded to the cats, and said,

> *"One of fire, two of light,*
> *Three from ground at dead of night.*
> *Four in strands of deep sea foam,*
> *Five that sings and brings them home."*

The cats stretched upward and dug their claws into the straw. With a faint *pop*, a spark of dim purple light appeared on the rim of the laundry basket. It rolled around the edge, then spread down along the sides to where Scorn and Trouble held on. The cats meowed in harmony, and the light winked out, leaving a smell of burned nutmeg.

"There," said Morwen. "Now, Killer—"

"Hurry!" said the donkey. "It's getting worse. Owww! None of the other things hurt like this."

"That doesn't surprise me," Morwen said after a quick look. "You're growing wings, and Telemain's lying across the top of them. Cimorene, give me a hand, please."

"Wings?" Killer sounded stunned. "Me?"

Trouble snickered. "A bright blue six-foot donkey with wings. What an idea."

Together, Morwen and Cimorene got Telemain off Killer's back and into the laundry basket. Killer sighed in relief as the weight lifted, then he craned his neck backward to get a look at his new appendages.

"They're awfully large," he said after a stunned moment.

"They're not just large," Cimorene said. "They're enormous."

"And they're still growing," Trouble pointed out.

"Fertilizer," Morwen said resignedly. "Magic fertilizer. I *thought* there'd be trouble over that hay."

"Can't you stop them?" Killer asked nervously.

"They'll stop growing on their own, when they run out of—of the fertilizer magic," Morwen said. "It shouldn't take too long. You didn't eat much of MacDonald's hay. Now, Kazul, if you'll let go of the rope and tell our future host to give it a tug—"

Fire ran down the rope from the window to the knot, then flared brightly and died. When Kazul opened her hand, the charred ends of the three short ropes fell into the laundry basket, along with a few horrible-smelling flakes of black ash. There was nothing left of the long rope. Above them, the window slammed shut.

Shaking her hand as if it stung, Kazul said, "I think he's changed his mind."

"Too late," Morwen said. "Trouble, Scorn, let's go."

"Do we get a raise?" Trouble asked as he leapt into the laundry basket.

"Move over," Scorn said, following.

"Morwen, what are you going to do?" Cimorene asked in a worried tone.

"Get Telemain inside where it's warm and dry," Morwen replied. "I'll send the basket back for you and Killer."

"Are you sure you should—"

"I'm sure." Morwen settled herself against the side of the laundry basket and took hold of the rim. Tapping three times with her left forefinger, she said, "Onward and upward."

The laundry basket shuddered, then slowly began to rise. Morwen made no attempt to speed it up. The broomstick spell was stretched a little thin as it was. As they passed Kazul's nose, Trouble stuck a long gray paw over the rim and waved. The laundry basket wobbled in response, and Trouble scrambled back toward the center.

"Hold still," Morwen told him. "You could dump us over if you aren't careful. This isn't a broomstick."

"Now she tells me."

"I should think it was obvious."

To this Trouble made no reply. Morwen sat motionless, watching the pale surface of the tower glide past. Finally, the laundry basket reached the window. "Stop," said Morwen.

The laundry basket obliged. Peering in, Morwen saw a thin young man with bright red hair standing beside a fireplace, his back to the window. *A fire-witch?*

thought Morwen. *In the middle of a swamp?* Well, not all red-haired people were fire-witches. Morwen glanced around the rest of the room. On the far side, a staircase led downward next to the wall. A stone bench, a small desk, and three comfortable-looking chairs were the only furnishings.

With great care, Morwen leaned forward and tapped on the glass. The young man jumped and whirled, and his eyes got very large. When he did not come any nearer, Morwen tapped the window again.

"Just break it," said Trouble. "It would be less work."

Scorn snorted. "You are thinking about as much as that blue winged imbecile down below. If she breaks the window, some of the glass might fall on top of them." She waved her tail at the figures of Kazul, Telemain, Cimorene, and Killer beneath them. "She can't count on *all* of it falling inside, even if she's careful."

For the third time, impatiently, Morwen rapped at the window. The red-haired man blinked, as if he were coming out of a daze, and then walked over to the window.

"Who are you?" he said, his voice slightly muffled by the glass.

"My name is Morwen, and I have an injured friend here who needs rest and warmth. Open this window immediately, please."

"I suppose I might as well." The redhead unlatched the window and swung it open, narrowly missing Morwen's head. "Sorry."

"And well you should be," Morwen told him. "Are you always so careless?"

"Mostly," said the man. "How did you get up—

That's my laundry basket!" He stared for a moment, then hit his forehead with the palm of his hand. "Stupid, stupid, stupid. You enchanted the basket. Why didn't *she* think of that years ago? Why didn't *Rachel* think of it? Why in heaven's name didn't *I* think of it?"

"Because you're stupid?" Scorn suggested.

"When I think of all the effort I could have saved, hauling that thing up and down and up and down and—"

"Yes, of course," said Morwen. "Now, if you could just give me a hand with—Trouble! Not yet." The cat had crouched, preparing to spring out of the laundry basket.

"What's that?" said the man. "What sort of trouble? And why do you want a hand with it?"

"Cats," said Morwen. "And I don't want a hand with them. It's Telemain who—"

As if the sound of his name had partially awakened him, Telemain grunted and stirred. The laundry basket swung sideways, throwing Trouble off his feet. This made the basket swing even more wildly. Morwen bent forward and grabbed the window ledge, which helped stabilize things a little. Then Telemain moaned and tried to sit up. The laundry basket wobbled violently, nearly spilling everyone out. The cats wailed, and Morwen was only just able to keep hold of the window ledge.

"Blast the man!" Morwen said. "Why does he have to pick just this instant to start recovering? Telemain, hold *still*."

The red-haired man leaned out of the window and grabbed the rim of the laundry basket. "Stop that immediately," he said sternly. "Stay *put*."

The laundry basket froze. Trouble yowled and leapt from the bottom of the laundry basket to the young man's bent-over back, and from there into the room. "Good idea," said Scorn, and followed.

"Oof! Oof!" said the man. "What was that?"

"Cats," Morwen said again. "Help me get Telemain out of here before he dumps us over."

Between the two of them, they wrestled Telemain out of the laundry basket and through the window. To Morwen's mild surprise, the basket remained perfectly stable throughout the entire operation, but as soon as the red-haired man turned away the basket began to wobble once more.

"There's another person and an oversized donkey at the foot of your tower as well," Morwen said when Telemain was safely inside, lying comfortably on the floor in front of the fireplace. They'd have to wait to do anything about the mud that covered him from head to foot, but fortunately the red-haired man did not have much in the way of carpeting. The stone floor would sweep up easily enough. "I'd like to bring the others up as soon as possible. The donkey will be a bit tricky."

"I'll be glad to—" The young man broke off, and his expression darkened, as if he were remembering something that annoyed him. "No. I shouldn't have let you in. You had your chance."

Morwen looked at him sternly over the tops of her glasses. "If you are sulky because we didn't allow you to haul us up immediately, you are being unreasonable, unmannerly, and overly bad tempered, even for a fire-witch. Enchanting that basket of yours has saved you a good deal of effort, now and in the future, and you ought to thank us for it."

"How do you know I'm a fire-witch?" the man demanded angrily.

"You have red hair, a touchy disposition, and an instinctive control over magic, even other people's spells," Morwen said. "And from the way you burned that rope, you've some affinity for fire as well. It's obvious. Now, are you going to let me bring up those people or not?"

"I don't—"

"Morwen, company," said Scorn.

Morwen turned. Outside the open window, enormous wings flapping furiously, Killer was coming in for a landing. Cimorene lay low along his back to avoid the wings, her arms wrapped around his neck.

"Have you found something we can have for dinner?" Killer asked.

14

In Which They Trade Stories

The red-haired man stared at the apparition in disbelief. Morwen didn't blame him. Killer looked nearly as unsteady as the laundry basket, which was still hovering just outside the window.

"What on earth is that?" the man demanded.

"My friends," Morwen said. "You'd better back up. There's not much room to spare, coming through that window, and Killer's never done this before."

"Killer?" The man backed up hastily. "Good grief, it's *blue*."

"Oh, really?" said Scorn, her voice dripping sarcasm. "We hadn't noticed."

"You know, I don't think his wings will fit through the opening unless he folds them," Trouble said. "I wonder how he'll manage?"

Killer flapped higher, then dove for the window, folding his wings at the last minute. His momentum wasn't quite enough to carry him through, and for an instant his front hooves flailed uselessly against air inside the tower while his back legs hung outside. Then he kicked, wiggled, and tumbled into the room, where he sprawled six inches above the floor, panting loudly. The sudden jerk tore Cimorene loose, and she landed next to Killer with a thud.

"Ow!" said Cimorene. "Morwen, are you all right? When the basket didn't come down again, I got worried."

"Everything is fine," Morwen said. "Telemain is even beginning to come out of the initial stages of backshock."

"Then what took you so long?" Cimorene demanded.

"I was chatting with our host . . ." Morwen turned expectantly to the red-haired man.

"Brandel," the red-haired man supplied. He still sounded sullen, but there was an undercurrent of interest, too. "I suppose that, since you're in, you can stay." He looked from Morwen to Killer to the cats to Cimorene. "But you're going to have to explain yourselves."

"In a minute," Morwen said. "First, we have to tell Kazul what's been going on. Unless you want a worried dragon tearing your tower apart." Without waiting for Brandel to answer, she leaned out the window and began shouting reassurances.

Explaining to Kazul took some time, and after that they had to haul the laundry basket back inside. Once it was in, they discovered that Killer had kicked a hole in the side in his last desperate lunge through the window. This put Brandel out of sorts again.

"I should throw you all back out the window immediately," he grumbled. "You're nothing but a lot of vagabonds."

"That doesn't sound right," Killer said, climbing to his feet. "Unless *vagabonds* is a word for a witch and a magician and the Queen of the Enchanted Forest and the King of the Dragons and some cats. And me. Is that what it means, Morwen?"

"Not exactly. Brandel is just grouchy."

"Oh." Killer shook himself, which made his wings flop open. He had to flap them once to keep his balance and then again to get them back in position. "I thought having wings would be interesting, but they're just a big nuisance."

"What was that about queens and kings and magicians?" Brandel asked Morwen.

So Morwen made a round of formal introductions, which soothed everyone's feelings. Then, just when they were getting ready to sit down and talk, Telemain stirred again and Morwen had to quiet him.

"I thought you wanted him to wake up," Killer said.

"I do, but thrashing around won't help him recover," Morwen said. "He needs to keep quiet."

"No problem," said Trouble. He stood up, stretched, strolled over to Telemain, and draped himself down the center of the magician's chest. "How long do you want him like this?"

"Thank you, Trouble," Morwen said, feeling relieved. Not only would Trouble's efforts hasten Telemain's recovery, but keeping Telemain quiet would also keep Trouble from getting into trouble. Given a specific job, the cat was quite reliable. "Two or three more hours should do it, now that he's warm. Then we can wake him, feed him some broth, and put him to bed."

"I bet he won't want to go," said Scorn.

"Three hours. Right." Trouble yawned and put his head down on his paws.

"I thought regular witches were supposed to have black cats," said Brandel, looking from Trouble to Scorn. "Unless—are you a fire-witch, too?"

"No," said Morwen. "But I don't see why that should limit me to black cats."

Brandel started to ask something else, then stopped, frowning. "No. I'll ask you about that later. Right now, you're here and you're all settled, and I want my explanation. Before something *else* happens."

"First, I'd like to know how you feel about wizards," Morwen said.

"I've never met one," Brandel replied. "And I'm not sure I want to. They don't have a very good reputation."

"Good," said Cimorene. "It's like this . . ." And she launched into the explanation.

Brandel listened with interest, but when Cimorene reached the end of her tale, he frowned. "How did you get by the invisible dusk-blooming chokevines? I thought I'd gotten all the openings near the tower filled in."

"Kazul burned a path through them."

"Mmph. Must be handy, traveling with a dragon."

"Sometimes," said Morwen. "Other times it's an inconvenience."

Suddenly, Scorn's ears pricked up and her whiskers twitched forward. "Well, *well*. What's this?"

Morwen glanced sideways to see what Scorn was watching so intently. On the top step of the staircase, a large, fluffy cat stood gazing at the newcomers. He was mostly black, with a white chin, white front paws, and a white tuft at the very end of his tail, and his expression was wary and disapproving.

"So you've finally decided to come see what was going on, have you?" Brandel said to the cat.

"Mrrow," said the cat.

"We have visitors," Brandel said. "Morwen, Cimorene, Killer, this is my cat, Horatio."

"Well, hel-lo, handsome," said Scorn. Her tail lashed once each way, and she sat up and began washing her face with great unconcern.

"He doesn't look that great to me," Trouble snarled.

"Behave yourself," Morwen said sternly. "We're guests."

Horatio eyed the group a moment longer, then came slowly forward. Halfway across the room, he stopped, studying Scorn with an intensity that matched hers. "Mmmrrr," he said at last. "Mrow yow eiou?"

"No, she won't!" Trouble shifted uneasily, as if longing to jump up and pounce on this intruder. Then Morwen caught his eye, and he settled back into place on Telemain's chest, muttering under his breath.

Scorn looked from Trouble to Horatio and made a show of considering. "You don't need me for anything right now, do you Morwen?"

"No," said Morwen.

"Then I'll be happy to look around," Scorn said to Horatio. "See you later, folks."

"Watch your step," Trouble growled. "You can't trust him."

"I should hope not," said Scorn. "After all, he's a cat." Tail high, she sauntered over to Horatio. The two cats exchanged sniffs, then Horatio led the way to the staircase and they disappeared.

"She's going to regret this," Trouble said. "So is he, as soon as I—"

Morwen caught his eye again, and he stopped short. "I don't expect to have to warn you twice," she said.

"All right, all right, but you wait and see."

"Quiet," said Morwen. "Brandel, we've told you what *we're* doing here. Now suppose you tell us what *you're* doing here."

"Living," said Brandel. "Staying out of trouble. At least, that's how it was supposed to work," he added sourly.

"Of course," said Cimorene with considerably more patience than Morwen could have mustered. "But how did you come here in the first place? The middle of a swamp is an unusual place to find a fire-witch."

Brandel sighed. "It's a little complicated. I come from a family of fire-witches. Both my parents are fire-witches, and so are most of my aunts and uncles and cousins. My eldest sister is a fire-witch, and my younger brother. Everyone, in fact, except my younger sister, Rachel."

"That must have been difficult for her," Cimorene said. "Being the only different one in the family is hard."

"My parents thought the same thing," Brandel said. "So when Rachel was very small, Mother brought her to the sorceress who lived in this tower, to be apprenticed."

"A sorceress chose to live in a swamp?" Cimorene said skeptically.

"They like inaccessible places," Morwen said. "Though I'll grant you, this is a little extreme. Go on, Brandel."

"The sorceress agreed to take Rachel in and teach her magic, and once every five years or so we would come and visit. Since there wasn't a door in the tower, the sorceress lowered a chair on a long rope and hauled us up to the window one at a time." Brandel shook his head. "The laundry basket is a lot safer; it's not so easy to fall out of.

"In any case, the sorceress asked us to keep the arrangement a secret, and we tried, but that sort of thing always seems to get out somehow. Some of the rumors were pretty wild: one of the stories said my mother sold Rachel to a wicked witch in exchange for some vegetables."

"I think I've heard that one," Cimorene said.

"Anyway, there wasn't much we could do. By the time Rachel was sixteen, all sorts of people were showing up in the swamp to rescue the beautiful princess from the wicked witch."

Cimorene nodded. "I know what that's like. When I was Kazul's princess, the knights and heroes made themselves a dreadful nuisance. You wouldn't believe how stubborn some of them could be."

"Want to bet? They're still coming around, and half the time they won't listen when I say she isn't here any longer." Brandel looked down. "That's what I thought you were, at first: a group of heroes."

"Sounds like a reasonable description to me," said Trouble.

"*Is* your sister beautiful?" Morwen asked.

Brandel shrugged. "She's pretty enough, I suppose. For a while, she was flattered by all the attention, but the constant interruptions just irritated the sorceress. Finally, she gave the tower to Rachel and moved somewhere else, just to get away from it all."

"I can't say I blame her," Cimorene said, nodding.

"I don't know," said Killer, who had been listening with great interest. "It must have taken a lot of work to build a place like this. Couldn't she have just kept them away somehow?"

"They're very persistent," Cimorene said. "You have no idea."

"And besides, heroes weren't the only problem with this location," Brandel said. "Just the main one."

Killer snorted softly. "I still think—"

"About the tower," Morwen said to Brandel. "The sorceress gave it to your sister . . ."

"And she lived here for a while, until she couldn't stand having strangers stand outside and shout, 'Rachel! Rachel, send down the chair' any longer. Half the time they didn't even get her name right. So when Arona started making life difficult for me, she—"

Morwen stiffened. "Hold on a minute. *Who* did you just say was making life difficult for you?"

"Arona Vamist." Brandel's eyes narrowed and his fists clenched. "He is the meanest, lowest, most obnoxious, narrow minded, opinionated . . ." With every word Brandel's voice rose, until he was shouting at the top of his lungs. Then, abruptly, his hair burst into flames.

After a shocked instant, Morwen relaxed. Fire-witches were supposed to be immune to fire, among their many other gifts, and she found this demonstration extremely interesting. Cimorene, too, seemed more surprised than frightened, but Killer was not so sanguine. He reared back in surprise, forgot to allow for his wings, and almost overbalanced. To keep his footing, he had to flap several times, filling the room with the wind from his wings. The flames brightened briefly, but then the breeze distracted Brandel from his angry tirade, and a moment later his hair went out.

"That was interesting," said Trouble.

"Interesting isn't the half of it," said Morwen. "That wouldn't by any chance have been Arona Michaelear Grinogion Vamist you were railing at a moment ago, would it?"

"That's the one," Brandel said, nodding vehemently. "And if I ever get my hands on the sneaking little—"

"Yes, of course," Morwen interrupted hastily, hoping to forestall another outburst. "If talking about it won't upset you too much, would you mind telling me exactly how Arona Michaelear Grinogion Vamist was 'making life difficult' for you?"

"Not just for me. That weasel has it in for the whole family." The ends of Brandel's hair began to glow like embers in a high wind. With a visible effort, he controlled himself and went on. "He'd been going on about *true magic* and *traditional forms* for a long time, but nobody ever paid much attention. Then he petitioned the Town Council to outlaw all 'nontraditional' magic, and somehow he got them to do it."

"And fire-witches aren't on his traditional list," Morwen said.

Brandel nodded. "He got us thrown out of our home, and there wasn't a thing we could do about it."

"Nothing?" Cimorene raised an eyebrow. "From what I've heard about fire-witches—"

"Using our magic against him would only have made his arguments to the Town Council sound more reasonable," Brandel said.

Cimorene and Morwen just looked at him.

"All right, we tried!" Brandel hit the arm of his chair with one fist, and little flames flickered in his hair. "Somebody was helping the little creep. He has a really first-class protective spell, one the whole lot of us couldn't get a handle on. When we found out we couldn't get at him, the others went to visit my uncle in Oslett. I came here, hoping Rachel would know where the sorceress had gone. I thought maybe she'd help."

"Rachel didn't know, I take it?" said Morwen.

"No, but she let me have the tower. She even warned me about all the knights and heroes before she left, but I didn't believe her." Brandel sighed. "I do now. That's why I filled in the end of the sorceress's walkway."

"Walkway?" said Cimorene.

"The one lined with invisible dusk-blooming choke-vines. Didn't you notice?"

"We noticed the vines. We didn't notice a walk-way. Just mud."

Brandel shrugged. "I don't think she got out much, and when she did, she usually flew."

"So you've been living here ever since you got thrown out of your hometown?" Morwen asked.

Brandel nodded.

"How long is that?"

"Around four months, I think. I lose track. Not a lot happens, except knights, and the days sort of blur together. I don't even know what's been happening outside the swamp."

"Arona Michaelear Grinogion Vamist seems to have decided to move on from fire-witches to regular witches," Morwen said. "As near as I can tell, he's trying to get everyone to wear pointy hats and cackle a lot."

"You watch out," Brandel said. "He's up to something."

"I'm beginning to regret missing his call," Morwen said.

"*You* got a call from this Vamist person?" said Cimorene. "What did he want?"

"The cats didn't say."

Trouble let his eyelids close almost to slits. "Nothing important."

"That reminds me," Cimorene said. "Brandel, have you got a magic mirror around that I could use? I promised Mendanbar I'd let him know how things were going every once in a while."

"I think the sorceress left an old one in the storage closet," Brandel said. "I'll check."

The fire-witch disappeared down the staircase. Morwen and Cimorene looked at each other.

"This is *not* going well," Cimorene said.

"I wouldn't say that," Morwen replied. "We have somewhere dry to spend the night. Under the circumstances . . ."

"That's just it. The circumstances. We're goodness-knows-how-many leagues from where we ought to be, Telemain's hurt, and we still don't have any idea where Mendanbar's sword is. And we've wasted a whole day. Any minute now, that sword may start leaking magic, and—"

"—and fretting yourself into fits won't help a bit," Morwen said. "Magical pressure takes time to build up, and it's only been a day and a half since the sword was stolen. We probably have at least another day before the magic of the Enchanted Forest starts draining out."

"Probably. But what if we don't?"

Morwen sighed. "Perhaps we're approaching the problem from the wrong direction. Let me think about it."

"With Telemain to take care of, when will you have time?"

"I'll manage," Morwen said.

A muffled *thump* echoed from the stairwell. Another followed, then some scraping noises. "Ow!" said Brandel's voice. A moment later, the carved wooden rim of an enormous old mirror thrust up out of the stairwell.

"My goodness, it's large." Cimorene rose hastily and went over to help. "You should have said something."

"I'd forgotten how big it is," Brandel panted.

Together, they hoisted the mirror the last few feet

up the stairs and propped it against the wall. "Will it do?" Brandel asked.

"I don't see why not," Cimorene said, but she sounded doubtful.

Morwen couldn't blame her. The sorceress's magic mirror was so old that the glass had uneven areas that distorted the reflection. Tarnish mottled the silver backing like black moss, and the wooden frame had deep cracks.

"Well, there's no point in waiting," Cimorene said.

"Mirror, mirror, on the wall,
I would like to make a call."

Leaning forward, she waited eagerly for the mirror's response.

15

In Which They Have Difficulties with a Mirror

Slowly, the splotchy reflection of the room faded into a smooth, even white. Then a voice from the mirror said, "Really?" It sounded hoarse, as if it hadn't been used in a long time. "Are you sure you don't want to leave me down in that storeroom for another twenty or thirty years, gathering dust and cobwebs and talking to the magic cloaks for company? Not that I'm complaining, mind, but cloaks don't have much in the way of conversation."

"I wish to speak to Mendanbar, the King of the Enchanted Forest," Cimorene said firmly.

"You're supposed to specify that in the verse, you know," the mirror said. "Though I guess I can make an exception, this once. Especially since you know exactly who you want to talk to. None of this 'fairest of them all' silliness. I hate that. I have to hunt through seven or eight hundred people, and in the end it's a matter of opinion anyway, and nobody is ever happy with the results. Now, you are clearly a woman of decision. 'I wish to speak to Mendanbar, King of—' Wait a minute. King? Are you sure?"

"Quite sure," said Cimorene. "Put me through to him, please."

"If you insist," said the mirror, "but I should warn you that in my experience kings don't talk to just anyone."

"He'll talk to me. I'm his wife."

"Well, sorry, Your Majesty," said the mirror in a huffy tone. "I'll get right to it. I suppose you know that there's mud on your cheek."

Before Cimorene could reply, the mirror filled with slowly swirling colors, and from it came the sound of someone humming a soft melody ever-so-slightly off key. "Mirror!" said Cimorene. "Mirror?"

The mirror did not respond. "I think you just have to wait until it comes back," said Brandel.

"Isn't there some way to make it stop humming?" said Cimorene. "Morwen? You know about magic mirrors."

"Not enough to do that," Morwen said regretfully.

Finally, the humming stopped and the mirror cleared, but instead of the grinning face of the gargoyle in Mendanbar's study, or Mendanbar himself, they saw only the same milky whiteness as they had before. "I'm sorry," said the mirror. "I don't seem to be able to get through."

Cimorene and Morwen stared at the mirror for a moment in appalled silence. Then Cimorene said, "Can't get through? Why not?"

"How should I know? I'm just a mirror."

"Try again," said Morwen.

"And no humming this time!" Cimorene added, but she was too late. The swirling colors—and the humming—were back.

This time the wait seemed interminable. Cimorene paced back and forth in front of the mirror, frowning and biting her lower lip. Finally, the humming stopped and the mirror cleared.

"Nope," it said. "There's nothing to communicate with. Are you sure he has a magic mirror?"

"He did when we left," Cimorene said.

"Maybe someone broke it," Killer suggested.

"Unlikely, but possible," Morwen told him. "Still, I think the difficulty is probably at this end."

"There's nothing wrong with me!" said the mirror indignantly. "I've had no complaints, not one, in all the years since I was first enchanted."

"That was, however, a long time ago." Morwen turned to Cimorene. "Telemain did the spell on the mirror at the castle, didn't he?"

Cimorene nodded. "Last year, as a wedding present. He updated it just a few weeks ago."

"Then it is possible that the two mirrors are incompatible," Morwen said.

"Ridiculous," said the mirror. "I'm very easygoing. I get along with everyone, even that dreadful woman who spied on her stepdaughter all the time. Now, *that* woman was incompatible with everyone. Honestly, the things she did—"

"Go to sleep," Morwen said.

"Phooey," said the mirror, and the milk white surface faded back into blotchy silver.

"Do you really think it's just a problem with the different spells?" Cimorene asked doubtfully, but her expression had lightened a little already.

"It doesn't happen often, but it does happen," Morwen said. "We can ask Telemain about it tomorrow morning. Maybe he'll have some suggestions."

"I don't know." Cimorene chewed gently on her lower lip. "I think I need to talk to Kazul. Killer—"

"Oh no," said the donkey. "Not me. Flying is too much work. And I haven't had any dinner yet."

"He does sound like Fiddlesticks," said Trouble.

"I suppose I should get you something," Brandel said without much enthusiasm. "What would you like?"

Killer's eyes lit up. "Clover. With sweet flowers and slightly tart leaves, for a nicely balanced mix of flavors, and maybe a little parsley as a palate cleanser. Not the kind of parsley that crinkles up, the kind with the flat leaves."

"I'll see what I have," Brandel said, sounding slightly stunned.

"Well, if Killer won't help, I'll have to take the laundry basket," Cimorene said with a shrug. "Will you show me how to use it, Morwen?"

"Certainly," Morwen said. "Just bear in mind that the balance is a little tricky."

"It can't be any worse than the magic carpet Mendanbar and I had to ride when we were looking for Kazul," Cimorene replied. "I'll manage."

Morwen nodded, and she gave Cimorene the short

list of basket-control commands. Together, the two women wrestled the basket out the window and set it hovering. Then Morwen held it while Cimorene climbed carefully into it. To make sure nothing went wrong, Morwen watched as Cimorene started down, then she turned away from the window with a smile. Cimorene was right. She could manage.

A new series of thumps and scrapes echoed up the stairwell, and Brandel appeared, carrying a bushel basket heaped full of clover.

"Now, where did you find that?" Morwen asked.

"The sorceress didn't like running to town for groceries," Brandel said, setting the basket in front of Killer. "So she enchanted her pantry so it would always have whatever she needed, for herself or for any visitors who happened to stop by."

"I thought she didn't have visitors," Morwen said.

"She didn't have many. I suppose she thought having company was bad enough without having to go shopping to feed them, too."

Killer's ears stiffened, and he paused in midbite. "Enchanted?" he said around a mouthful of clover. "This is more enchanted food?"

"No, no, it's the *pantry* that's enchanted. The *food* is perfectly normal," said Brandel. "Weren't you listening?"

"You'll have to pardon him," Morwen said. "He's trying to be cautious because he's had a bad experience. A series of bad experiences."

"You're *sure* this is safe?" Killer said anxiously. "I'm getting tired of all these changes."

"It's a little late to worry about it now," Trouble

told him. "You've already eaten some. I don't suppose Brandel thought to bring a saucer of cream along with all that rabbit food?"

"Yes, about the rest of us . . . ," Morwen said.

"Oh, sorry." Brandel looked embarrassed. "I guess I'm not used to having company. What would you like?"

"Let's see what you have," said Morwen, and started for the stairs.

By the time Cimorene returned, Morwen and Brandel had laid out a substantial supper, including roast boar, baked potatoes, carrots, green beans and tiny onions, and spring water for the people; and sardines with cream for the cats. Killer had finished his first basket of clover, the second was half gone, and he was beginning to slow down. It looked as if he might, for once, have enough to eat at a meal.

"Did you have a nice chat with your dragon?" Brandel asked as Cimorene pushed the laundry basket into a corner where it would be out of the way.

Cimorene rolled her eyes. "Kazul is not, and never has been, *my* dragon. I was *her* princess for a while, but now we're just friends."

"Oh. Well, did you have a nice chat with your friend, then?"

"Sort of." Cimorene looked at Morwen. "Kazul is leaving."

Morwen considered. "When? And why?"

"Right away. She—"

Something large *whooshed* past the window outside. "There she goes," Cimorene said.

"That still leaves why." Morwen pulled a chair up to the table and sat down. "You can explain over dinner."

"Something smells good up here," Scorn said from the staircase, poking her black nose over the top of the last step. "Hey, Horatio, there's cream!"

"If I don't get any, I will be *very* upset," said Trouble, lashing his tail for emphasis as the other two cats bounded out of the stairwell and headed for the bowls Brandel had left on the floor.

Cimorene smiled absently at the cats and joined Morwen at the table. "It's—well, dragons aren't very patient at the best of times. And we haven't run into any wizards yet, and Kazul wasn't sure your enchanted pantry would be up to feeding a dragon. So since I was worried about Mendanbar—"

"And since Mendanbar said something about wizards in the Enchanted Forest when you talked to him last night—," Morwen said.

"And since there's not much dragon food in the swamp—," Killer put in.

"—Kazul offered to go home and—and see what's going on." Cimorene took a large helping of the roast boar and dug in with relish.

"It may be just as well." Morwen took a much smaller portion of the boar and looked at it doubtfully, wondering whether her stomach was up to it. "Once we have the sword, we'll want to return to the Enchanted Forest immediately. Telemain won't be fit for much for a day or so, but—"

"Oh no! Morwen, we can't afford to sit around here for a whole day!"

"If you have a better idea, I'd like to hear it," said

Morwen. "Besides, we haven't got the slightest idea where we're going, so rushing off won't get us there any quicker. We'll be better off if we take time to plan."

"I suppose so," Cimorene said, but she didn't sound happy about it.

"As I was saying: By tomorrow morning, I'll have some idea when Telemain will be able to do a proper transport spell again. Without Kazul, he can take us considerably farther each time and still stay within the safety limits."

Cimorene swallowed a mouthful of potato. "That's good. The faster we go, the sooner we'll get the sword back to the Enchanted Forest."

"Exactly." With some regret, Morwen set down her fork. "For tonight, the best thing we all can do is rest. Brandel, will you help us with Telemain?"

"I don't need help," Telemain said unexpectedly from the floor in front of the fire. "I need dinner. Where are we, and why is there a cat on my chest?"

"He was supposed to be making sure you stayed asleep," Morwen said, turning to give Trouble a reproving look.

"It's not *my* fault," Trouble said. "He doesn't react right. I've never had to use that spell on a magician before; maybe that's why." He rose and stepped carefully down from Telemain's chest. "Are there any sardines left?"

Telemain sat up and looked at Trouble with dislike. "That animal is remarkably heavy for something that looks that skinny."

"That's gratitude for you," said Trouble. "He should be glad I'm not Chaos."

"How are you feeling?" Cimorene asked Telemain anxiously.

"Squashed," said Telemain. "And may I point out that as yet no one has answered my first question. Where are we?"

"The Smoking Swamp," Morwen told him. "And this is Brandel. We were fortunate enough to find his tower in time to spend the night, or you'd be sleeping in mud."

"I appear to have done that already," Telemain said, picking flakes of dried mud from the left shoulder of his vest. Suddenly, he looked up, frowning. "Spend the *night?*"

"You got an unusually heavy dose of backshock when you lost control of the transportation spell," Morwen told him. "You've been unconscious all day."

"Ridiculous," said Telemain. "I did not lose control of the transportation spell, and I am not suffering from backshock."

"Well, this certainly isn't the edge of the Great Southern Desert," Cimorene said. "And *something* knocked you out for most of the day."

"I had to carry you," Killer said, bobbing his head up and down for emphasis. "You're heavy."

Morwen's eyes narrowed. "If it isn't backshock, what is it?"

"The opposite of backshock," Telemain said. "I don't believe there is a word for it."

"Explain."

"Backshock occurs when the accumulated magical energy contained within an enchantment-in-process rebounds upon the magician casting the spell due to his inability to maintain control," Telemain said.

"He's feeling better, all right," said Trouble, glancing up from the sardines.

"Mrrow vrow?" said Horatio.

"Yes," said Scorn. "Sometimes he's even worse."

"In this instance, both the disruption of the transportation spell and the prolonged unconsciousness that followed resulted from an expropriation of magical energy as a result of the partial absorption of my enchantment-in-process by a similar but much more extensive enchantment."

"What?" said Brandel.

"You're sure?" Morwen said, frowning.

"Positive," said Telemain. "The sensation was quite unmistakable. And I must also point out that the normal secondary consequences of backshock are not in evidence."

"What does *that* mean?" Cimorene said.

"It means I'm starving," Telemain said, climbing to his feet. "Can we finish this discussion over dinner?"

"Most of us have eaten," Morwen said. "You can have dinner while the rest of us discuss. About this other spell—"

"*What* other spell?" Cimorene said. "Morwen, will *one* of you please explain what you're talking about?"

"Sorry," Morwen said. "Telemain said that he didn't lose control of the transportation spell. Somebody else was transporting at the same time—"

"A very large somebody else," Telemain said, piling a plate with slices of roast boar and heaps of vegetables. "Or possibly someone moving a moderately large house."

"—and the second spell sucked up enough of Telemain's magic to break his spell right in the middle of things."

"Sucked up Telemain's magic?" Cimorene scowled. "That sounds an awful lot like wizards."

"Aren't you jumping to conclusions?" Brandel said. "I know wizards have a bad reputation, but they aren't *thieves*."

"They took Mendanbar's sword."

"And they've been stealing magic on a small scale for years," Morwen said. "Just ask the dragons."

"But if it *was* wizards, where were they going?" Cimorene tapped her fingers nervously against the arm of her chair. "And what were they planning to do when they got there? Oh, I *wish* I'd been able to reach Mendanbar."

Telemain made a questioning noise, so Morwen explained about Brandel's magic mirror. "I thought the spell might be incompatible with the one in the castle," she finished. "Do you feel up to checking, once you're done eating?"

"I can certainly try," Telemain said. "If that's the problem, though, I doubt that I'll be able to do anything about it until tomorrow. It takes time to rebuild magical reserves."

But when Telemain examined the mirror, he shook his head. "It's an old universal-application single-unit enchantment. Quite an impressive antique, and I can see that it's been well maintained. The connective interface is pretty basic, therefore—"

"Can you fix it to get through to Mendanbar or not?" Cimorene asked.

"I was getting to that." Telemain looked at the expression on Cimorene's face and sighed. "I'm afraid it doesn't need adjusting," he said with unusual gentleness. "There's nothing wrong with the spell, and it shouldn't be incompatible with the castle mirror. The problem is somewhere else."

"I knew it," Cimorene said. She rose and began to pace in front of the fireplace. "Something is wrong at home."

16

In Which They Learn Something Worth Knowing

Both Morwen and Telemain agreed with Cimorene, at least in part, but even if they had wanted to, they could not have done anything that night. Telemain was much too drained to cast another transportation spell, and they had no other way of getting back to the Enchanted Forest in a hurry. Furthermore, there was not much point in going back without the sword.

"Mendanbar has all the magic of the Enchanted Forest to use against the wizards," Morwen said. "He doesn't need more magicians. He needs his sword, so he can stop all of the wizards at once instead of attacking them one or two at a time."

"Yes, but there are so *many* of them," Cimorene said. "And there's only one of him. And what if the sword has started draining magic out of the forest? The wizards will be getting more powerful and Mendanbar will be getting less."

"If the sword has started leaking Enchanted Forest magic, the best thing we can do is to get it back to the forest quickly," Morwen said.

"And anyway, there are only three of us," Telemain pointed out. "That wouldn't change the odds much."

"There are six of us," Trouble said indignantly. "What's the matter, can't he count?"

"I'll admit that the rabbit isn't good for much, even as a donkey," Scorn said. "*We*, however, are another matter entirely."

"Kazul will be far more help to Mendanbar than we would," Morwen told Cimorene. "Our job is to get hold of that sword. And you are the only one who can do that."

Cimorene sighed. "I know. I just wish I could be there with him."

"Then we had better stop worrying about what Mendanbar is doing and start figuring out how to find his sword in the shortest possible time, so we get back as soon as we can," Morwen said.

Everyone agreed that this was an excellent idea, but though they discussed the matter for another hour, no one had any suggestions. Finally, Morwen put an end to the discussion. "We are all getting too tired to think," she said. "We will do much better in the morning." Brandel supplied them each with a room and a warm bath—which the cats declined—and Morwen made certain that the others were settled in before she retired herself.

The following morning, Morwen rose early. Even so, Telemain was up before she was. She found him in the topmost room of the tower, sitting in front of the dead ashes of the fire and staring at Brandel's magic mirror with an expression of concentration on his face. On the far side of the room, Killer slept with his head down and his oversized wings flopped awkwardly across his back.

"Good morning," Morwen said as she climbed the last few stairs. "How are your magic levels?"

"Much better," Telemain said absently. "Morwen, how much do you know about these old universal-application units?" He waved at the mirror.

"Using them or enchanting them?"

"Using them."

"Quite a bit," Morwen said. "Forty years ago they were standard equipment for witches, and learning to use them is still considered part of a witch's basic education. Why?"

"How universal is the universal application?" Telemain asked.

"It depends on the mirror. Can't you figure it out from looking at the underlying enchantment?"

Telemain frowned. "Probably, but it's not a good idea to take a working antique apart unless you absolutely have to. They're old and fragile, and if I popped one of the main core links it could take days to repair."

Morwen suppressed a sigh of irritation. There was no point in snapping at Telemain when he was in this mood. He wouldn't notice. "It would help if you told me what you want to do with it."

"I was considering the possibility of using the mirror as a locating device," Telemain said. "If the universal-application portion of the enchantment is truly universal . . ."

". . . then we can use it to find Mendanbar's sword," Morwen said. "What an excellent suggestion. I should have thought of it myself. Back at the castle, perhaps, when it would have saved us some time."

"It wouldn't have done any good then." Telemain bent over the mirror, oblivious to Morwen's sarcasm. "The enchantment on the castle mirror is limited to animate, sentient beings, and while Mendanbar's sword is occasionally temperamental, it is neither animate nor sentient. Now, if you'll just show me where the external connectors are, I'll hook this to a low-level identification spell and—"

"If all you want to do is find Mendanbar's sword, you shouldn't need an identification spell. The mirror is quite capable of handling the whole thing itself, if it's approached correctly."

"Who's approaching what, and why do you have to be correct about it?" Cimorene asked, climbing the last few stairs into the room. Trouble, who seemed to have been escorting her, bounded over the last step and stopped dead in his tracks. Cimorene did not quite trip over him, but it was a near thing.

"Telemain wants to use Brandel's mirror to find the sword," Morwen said, giving Trouble a reproving look. Trouble looked away and wandered casually toward Killer, who raised his head and blinked sleepily at the cat.

Dubiously, Cimorene examined the mirror. "Can it do that?"

"I see no reason why not," Morwen said. "You heard what it said last night about hunting for the fairest in the land. If it can do that, it ought to be able to look for a sword."

"Good," said Cimorene.

"Mirror, mirror, on the wall,
I would like to make a call."

Nothing happened. "What's the matter?" said Cimorene. "Is it broken?"

"Possibly," Telemain said. "Antique spells are easily disrupted."

"They're also cranky," said Morwen. Stepping forward, she tapped the mirror briskly on the left side.

Immediately, the mirror turned white, as if someone had thrown a large bucket of milk at the reverse side. "Now what?" it said, sounding extremely cross.

"I want to see where Mendanbar's sword is," Cimorene told it.

"Too bad," said the mirror. "I told you yesterday, that has to be specified in the verse. Get it right, or don't bother asking. I really can't make any more exceptions." Without waiting for an objection, the mirror turned its usual blotchy silver.

"Come back here!" said Cimorene, but the mirror remained obstinately silver.

"Hmph," said Morwen. "I suppose I should have expected this. My first magic mirror used to be irritable in the mornings, too."

"What can we do about it?" Cimorene asked.

"Give me a minute to think."

"I could constrain a certain level of performance," Telemain said, frowning. "However, the accuracy of the information obtained might leave something to be desired. On the other hand—"

"Better think fast," Trouble said to Morwen.

Footsteps sounded in the stairwell. "You're all up early," said Brandel. "Would you like some breakfast?"

"I'd like your blasted mirror to cooperate," Cimorene muttered under her breath.

"Got it," Morwen said. "Move over, Cimorene.

"Mirror, mirror, on a hook,
Where's the sword the wizards took?"

As the mirror's surface reluctantly faded to white, Telemain stared at Morwen in disbelief. "You call that a spell?"

"It rhymes and it scans," Morwen said. "What more do you want at this hour of the morning? And on the spur of the moment, too."

"I agree with him," the mirror said. "That was a *lousy* couplet."

"If you'd found us the sword to begin with, you wouldn't have had to listen to it," Morwen said, unperturbed. "Do your job."

Cimorene leaned forward. "And this time, please don't—"

Whirling colors filled the mirror, and a soft but penetrating off-key hum echoed through the room.

"—hum," Cimorene finished, half a second too late. "Bother!"

"As long as it finds the sword for us, I don't care if it sings an aria backward," Morwen said. "If it annoys you that much, put your fingers in your ears."

Trouble jumped onto the window ledge and curled

his tail around his feet. Two seconds later, Scorn and Horatio tore out of the stairwell and raced around the room, startling Killer into wakefulness. A loud bray drowned out the mirror's humming, and Brandel winced. As the cats settled onto various pieces of furniture for their morning wash, Cimorene nudged Morwen's side. "Look! It's working."

Morwen turned back to the mirror and smiled in satisfaction. The glass had cleared to show a large, ramshackle house with two chimneys and a steeply pointed roof. The windows were made up of small glass rectangles, and ivy covered most of them so thickly that it seemed unlikely that anyone could see out.

"*That's* the central office of the Society of Wizards?" Cimorene said.

"No," Telemain replied. "Apparently I was wrong, and they aren't keeping the sword at the central office. It's a good thing I thought to check." He sounded extremely smug. "Now all we have to do is find out where that house is."

"It's about five miles past the edge of the swamp," Brandel said. "Right outside the town where I grew up. But I don't think knowing that does you much good."

"Why do you say that?" Morwen asked.

"Because you said the Society of Wizards stole this sword you're after. *That* house belongs to Arona Michaelear Grinogion Vamist."

"What?"

"You mean it's the wrong *place?*" Cimorene said. "After all that?"

"It is *not* the wrong place!" the mirror said indignantly. "I've been a magic mirror for one hundred and forty-seven years, and I haven't made a mistake yet. Look here!"

The scene in the glass swooped and whirled dizzyingly, and then the view plunged through one of the ivy-covered windows into a dimly lit room. Inside, two men sat at a dusty table, drinking black coffee and contemplating a shiny sword lying on the table between them. One of them was bald and sharp faced, while the other—

"That's Antorell!" Cimorene said. "He's gotten himself back together awfully fast this time. It must be all the practice he's had."

"That's Arona!" Brandel said at the same instant, staring at the bald man. "Is that the sword you're looking for?"

"It appears to be," said Telemain.

Cimorene nodded. "That's Mendanbar's sword, all right. See how it looks twice as bright as anything else? I bet it's leaking magic all over."

"Leaking magic?" said Killer, poking his long nose over Morwen's shoulder to peer at the mirror. "You never said anything about that sword leaking magic. It doesn't sound very safe."

"It isn't," Cimorene told him. "Which is another reason why we have to get it back to the Enchanted Forest quickly. The longer it's outside the forest, the worse it gets. That sword *belongs* in the Enchanted Forest."

"Don't worry about it," Morwen said to Killer. "It won't hurt you unless you try to eat it."

"That would be fun to watch," said Trouble, cocking his head to one side.

"Mrow?" said Horatio.

"Probably not," Scorn said with some regret. "Even Killer isn't *that* stupid."

Brandel was still staring at the mirror with a grim expression. "So that's it. That no-good, interfering, lousy little troublemaking weasel has gotten the Society of Wizards to help him!" His voice rose steadily until he was shouting, and on "troublemaking" his hair burst into flames.

"Yow!" said Killer, jumping backward. "Ouch! That was my *ear*. Whoops!" As he recoiled from Brandel's blazing head, his wings flopped open, catching air and throwing him off balance. Twisting frantically to keep his left wing tip away from the fire, Killer flapped twice and fell over in a tangle of legs and ears and feathers. The cats bounced away from him, startled and bristling.

"Hey, watch what you're doing," said Scorn. "You could hurt someone." Horatio gave her neck a reassuring lick.

Slowly, Killer settled his wings into place and climbed back to his feet. "I think I sprained something," he said mournfully. "And my ear is singed." He gave Brandel a reproachful look.

Brandel didn't notice. Hair still burning merrily, he turned to Cimorene. "If you want some help getting that sword back, just ask. That sneaking, repulsive little—"

"Are you done?" asked the mirror. "Or do you actually want to watch these two have breakfast?"

"Possibly," said Morwen. "Telemain, is there any way we can hear what they're saying?"

"I doubt it," Telemain said. "In any event, it would require considerable time to determine the precise adjustments appropriate to the subcategory. Antiques are not my area of specialization."

"Watch who you're calling antique, buster," the mirror said. "I'll have you know that I found that sword in less than half the time it'd take some of your new-fangled hotshot mirrors."

"And a good job you did of it," Morwen said. "We're finished. Go to sleep."

" 'Antique,' " muttered the mirror as the reflection faded into white and then cleared to show the tower room once more. "Bah phooey to 'antique.' I'm just as good as I was a hundred years ago. Better! I've got more experience. *And* I give personal service. 'Antique!' Some people . . ."

"I think he hurt her feelings," Scorn said.

"What about *my* feelings?" Killer said loudly. "My ear is burned, I've bent three feathers and pulled a muscle in my back, and I'm *hungry*."

"So are the rest of us," Trouble said. "But you don't hear *us* complaining." He glanced at Scorn and Horatio, and then all three cats looked up at the humans with matching expressions of starvation being nobly borne in a good cause.

Morwen sighed. "Brandel, would you be good enough to calm down, stop flaming, and see about a morning meal? Or if you'd rather not be bothered, at least tell us how to work the pantry spell?"

Setting up breakfast took nearly half an hour, mostly because everyone except Killer and the cats had other preoccupations. Brandel and Cimorene kept getting sidetracked into a discussion of Arona Michaelear Grinogion Vamist and his involvement with the Society of

Wizards and the theft of the sword. Telemain was more interested in studying the mirror than in talking or food, and Morwen made a mental note to make sure he didn't skip breakfast. Backshock or not, he was still recovering, and he'd be a great deal more use if he ate well before they left. Morwen herself would have liked to join either Cimorene's discussion or Telemain's investigation, but for the most part she forced herself to stay out of them. After all, *someone* had to keep the others moving.

Finally, everything was ready, and they sat down to eat. "I still can't believe it," Brandel said, tipping three sausage patties onto his plate and handing the platter to Cimorene. "Vamist never liked the idea of wizards. They weren't traditional enough for him."

"Don't start on that again," Morwen said. "You'll use up all your energy burning your hair."

Cimorene swallowed a bite of toast and said, "Yes, what we need now is a plan. Can you give us directions to this Vamist person's house, Brandel?"

"I'll do better than that. I'll show you." Brandel scowled and a wisp of smoke rose out of his hair. "The idea of that pompous, overbearing skunk helping wizards after he got *us* kicked out of town for being non-traditional . . ."

"I wonder what they offered him?" Telemain said.

"How about a warding spell powerful enough to protect him from half a dozen fire-witches?" Morwen suggested.

"You mean he was working with them all along?" Brandel said. "That little—"

"We don't know that for certain," Cimorene said hastily. "Yet. And if you still can't go home, you can come back to the Enchanted Forest with us after we get the sword. I'm sure Mendanbar would be happy to have you, and the rest of your family, too."

"It's *lots* nicer than a swamp," Killer put in. "There's plenty of clover—at least, there's plenty for rabbits. I don't know if there's enough for six-foot donkeys with wings." His ears drooped at the thought.

"We'll worry about that later," Morwen told him. "Eat your breakfast. Brandel, how long will it take us to get to Vamist's house? And does anyone have any suggestions as to how we should proceed once we get there?"

"That's easy," Cimorene said. "It looked like Vamist and Antorell were the only ones there. Brandel and Telemain can go to the front door and distract them while you and I sneak in through the back and grab the sword. And if Antorell tries to stop me, I'll melt him. Pass the salt, please."

17

In Which There Is Much Excitement

Although they discussed the matter for the rest of the meal, Cimorene's plan was the best idea they had. Since only Cimorene could carry the sword, she had to be the person who sneaked in and took it. Morwen had to go with her because the cats were going to act as lookouts and no one else could understand them. Brandel was the logical person to distract Arona Vamist, and Telemain had to be with him in order to melt any wizards who might show up.

"What about me?" asked Killer.

"You get to stand outside the back door and stay out of mischief," Morwen told him. "You'd be safer here, but we'll probably want to transport home right from Vamist's house."

"You're *sure* you can manage that part, Telemain?" Cimorene asked.

"Quite certain," Telemain said a little crossly. "The last error was due to a cross-matrix interference that is not at all likely to be repeated."

"I might agree with you if we knew exactly what caused the interference in the first place," Morwen said. "Since we don't . . ."

"If it will make you feel better, I'll put a screening mechanism in the bypass module." This time, Telemain made no attempt whatsoever to hide his annoyance.

"Temperamental, isn't he?" said Scorn.

"A screening mechanism sounds like a very good idea to me," Morwen told Telemain. "And we aren't questioning your competence, so stop frowning. Getting the sword back to the Enchanted Forest is too important to take chances, even small ones."

"Then you'd better help me figure out what kind of adjustments to make to the springbase loader so that it won't ignore Brandel," Telemain said. "Since I assume you don't want to leave him behind for the wizards."

Brandel looked at Telemain with alarm. "Leave me behind? Why?"

"Fire-witches are immune to most spells," Morwen said. "Including ordinary transportation spells. Telemain is quite right; if we don't make a few changes, you'll undoubtedly find yourself standing alone in the middle of Arona Michaelear Grinogion Vamist's yard when the spell goes off."

"We can't let that happen!" Cimorene said. "If the Society of Wizards catches him, they'll do something awful."

"But you just said he's immune to spells," Killer said in a puzzled tone. "So what can the wizards do to him?"

"Break his legs, tie him to a tree for the nightshades to eat, stick him in a dungeon with no food," said Trouble. "Wizards don't need magic to do nasty things."

Horatio hissed. Killer's ears went stiff and the hair along his neck bristled. "No food! They wouldn't. Not really."

"Yes, they would," said Morwen. "*If* they caught him. Which they won't, because before we leave here, Telemain and I are going to make sure the transportation spell works on Brandel."

Killer bobbed his head up and down in vigorous agreement. "That's good. We don't want to leave anyone behind. No food! Those wizards really *are* horrible."

"You two work on the spell," Cimorene said. "I'll get everything else ready to go. How far away did you say this place is, Brandel?"

"Two or three hours' walk," Brandel said. "It'll take us an hour or so to get out of the swamp, but after that it should be easy."

Trouble lowered his head and lashed his tail in disgust. "More mud. And no dragon to ride on this time, either."

"Dibs on Morwen's shoulder," said Scorn.

"Mrrow!" said Horatio in an emphatic tone.

"Will you need me for the changes you want to make in the transportation spell?" Brandel asked Telemain. "Because if you won't, I'd like to make a few calls. The rest of the family ought to know that the Society of Wizards is behind Vamist."

Telemain removed a silver globe the size of a tennis ball from the pouch at his belt and studied it. "What? Yes, of course. Go ahead. Morwen, I think we should start with the shift alignment linkages. We'll have to add two or three interrupt vectors, and we may have to modify the invisible channel connection as well."

"We'll need you when we test our work," Morwen said to Brandel, "but that won't be until we're finished. You'll have plenty of time for your calls; this will take at least half an hour, possibly more."

Brandel nodded and left. Morwen turned back to Telemain. "I don't see the point of adding interrupt vectors. All we really need is a temporary change in the definition section so that it includes fire-witches."

Telemain's face went blank for a moment as he considered the idea. Then his nose wrinkled and his mouth twisted as if he had bitten into something very sour. "Temporary changes. How inelegant."

"As long as it's effective, who cares? Think of it as a trial run. You can study the ways all the various pieces interact, and do a permanent redesign later."

"True." The magician began to look more cheerful. "In that case, where do *you* suggest we start?"

Changing the transportation spell was simple, compared to keeping Telemain from putting in various extra things he wanted to test. Morwen insisted on doing the last few checks, since she was still a little worried about Telemain's condition. When they were sure everything worked properly, they called Cimorene, who had vanished down the stairwell while they were working.

"Coming." A moment later, Cimorene appeared at the head of the stairs, carrying her pack over her left shoulder and a long-handled straw broom in her right hand. "Morwen, have you got any of that flying ointment left? Because if you do, I think you should use it on this. We'll get to Vamist's house a lot faster if we don't have to slog through all that mud."

"I am *not* riding on that thing," Telemain said. "Mud or no mud."

"He wouldn't say that if *he'd* spent most of yesterday wading through the stuff," Scorn observed.

"You should talk," said Trouble. "Between riding on Morwen's shoulder and riding on Kazul's back, you never even got your paws dirty."

"I was going to suggest that you and Brandel ride in the laundry basket anyway," Cimorene said to Telemain. "There isn't room for all of us on the broomstick."

"There's a flying mortar and pestle in the basement," Brandel offered. "It's too heavy to use every day, and it's a little small, but if you'll help me haul it upstairs you can use it."

"It sounds nearly as uncomfortable as a broomstick," Telemain said. "No, thank you. I'll take the laundry basket."

"What about *us?*" Trouble demanded.

"You will come on the broomstick, where I can keep an eye on you," Morwen told him as she fished in her sleeve for the jar of flying ointment. "Scorn and

Horatio should probably go in the laundry basket, or possibly on Killer's back. We don't want to overload anything."

"I don't know," Killer said, ruffling his wings nervously. "I still don't like cats. And they've got *claws*."

"You bet we do." Trouble held up a paw and flexed it, displaying five wickedly curved and sharply pointed claws.

Killer shuddered. "Couldn't I go by myself?"

"No," Cimorene said firmly. "We all have to do what we can, and what you can do is carry the cats."

"Well, I'm not doing any more flying," Killer said, planting his feet for emphasis. "It's too hard, and it scares me."

"I bet he gets airsick, too," said Scorn. "Rabbits!"

While Morwen enchanted the broomstick, Brandel picked up the laundry basket and shoved it through the open window. Cimorene set it hovering and helped steady it as the two men climbed in. Then she sent Killer and the two cats out after the basket and turned to Morwen and Trouble.

"All done," Morwen said. "I hope the laundry basket holds together, because that was the last of the flying ointment."

"Then let's go. We don't want Telemain and Brandel to get too far ahead of us."

"Not to mention that rabbit," Trouble said.

They climbed onto the broomstick and took off. Cimorene had to duck as they went through the window.

"Excuse me, Cimorene," Morwen said as they swooped out and down. "I forgot how tall you are."

"Better watch for low branches," Trouble said.

"There aren't any low branches," Morwen told him, setting the broomstick to fly about ten feet off the ground.

A moment later, they caught up with Killer and the laundry basket, and the whole group continued on together. Their speed was limited to Killer's trotting pace, but with all the trees to dodge they could not have traveled much faster, even without him. Following Brandel's directions, they reached the edge of the swamp in fifteen minutes.

"It's straightforward from here," Brandel said. "Head west, toward those hills. At this rate, we should be there within half an hour."

"Half an hour!" Killer shook his mane, drawing yowls of protest from Scorn and Horatio. "You want me to keep running like this for another half an *hour?* I can't do it. And don't ask me to fly. That's even more work."

"Maybe if you didn't eat so much you'd be in better shape," Scorn said.

"Hrmrrrr," agreed Horatio.

"I do not!" said Killer. "It's all very well for the rest of you. *You* all get to ride. I want a rest and a drink and a snack to keep my strength up."

Morwen landed the broomstick. "That sounds reasonable enough, if you don't take too long. Five minutes now, and we'll stop again halfway there." She looked at Cimorene, who was frowning impatiently.

"I suppose we don't have much choice," Cimorene said. "And it really isn't fair to make Killer work so hard when it's so easy for the rest of us. But I do wish there were some way to—to speed things up. I'm worried about what those wizards might be doing at home."

"I'll think about it," Morwen said. "Now, as long as we're stopping for a few minutes . . . Killer, are there any invisible dusk-blooming chokevines around?"

"I can see two of them right over there." Killer pointed with his right ear. "Are you going to let me eat one?"

"No, I'm going to collect them for my garden," Morwen said. "Goodness knows when I'll get another chance." She began rummaging in her sleeves for a trowel and some specimen bags.

"Is this an appropriate time to be gathering plants?" Telemain said.

"We've promised Killer a five-minute rest. I may as well use the time constructively. You're going to analyze Brandel's magic again, aren't you?"

Telemain glanced at Brandel and shifted uncomfortably. "Given the necessity of a transportation spell and the possibility of unpredictable interactions between it and fire-witch magic, it seems wise to repeat—"

"Then don't fuss about my plants." Morwen turned to Killer. "Show me exactly where the vines are, and I'll give you the last bottle of cider. Don't get too close; they're dangerous, remember."

"How are you going to collect them, then?" Killer asked.

"Watch."

Puzzled but willing, Killer described the exact positions of the two chokevines. Cautiously, Morwen edged closer, until Killer said she was just within three feet of the plants. Then she stopped and took a spray bottle and a paper packet of powdered slowstone from her right sleeve.

"What's that?" Cimorene asked, interested in spite of herself.

"The bottle is plain water." Morwen pumped the top to get the spray working, then aimed it at the tree in front of her and covered as much as she could reach with a fine mist. Shining drops of water collected in midair, outlining invisible leaves and stems that shifted restlessly as if trying to reach Morwen and her friends.

"That's pretty," said Killer.

"That's wet," growled Trouble, shaking his fur as if he were the one who had been sprayed.

Morwen slipped the spray bottle back into her sleeve, then carefully opened one corner of the packet. Checking the direction of the wind, she shifted position until the slight breeze came from behind her, blowing toward the invisible dusk-blooming chokevines. "Everyone else, stay back," she said, and sprinkled the slowstone over the vines.

The gray powder settled over the dampened leaves, outlining them even more clearly than before. Slowly, the restless movement of the plants died down, until it was only a sluggish tremor. Morwen smiled in satisfaction. She hadn't been altogether certain that slowstone would work the same way on plants as it did on animals and people.

"What was that?" Telemain asked, breaking off his conversation with Brandel in midsentence.

"Powdered slowstone," Morwen said.

"It smells good," Killer said. "Like fresh dandelion greens with cinnamon bark."

"You wasted powdered slowstone on a couple of *plants?*" Telemain sounded completely outraged.

"I had to do something to calm them down," Morwen said. "This should keep them quiet for a day or two—long enough to transplant them in my garden, at any rate."

"Does that mean they're safe now?" Killer asked.

"Temporarily," Morwen replied, reaching for her trowel. "That is, they won't bother you if you get close, but I wouldn't eat them if I were you."

"Oh." Killer's ears drooped. "Why not? They smell awfully good, especially with that powdered stuff all over them."

"Weren't you listening at all?" Scorn said with a superior sniff. " 'That powdered stuff' is slowstone. It's magical, and it does just what it sounds like it ought to do. We'd be lucky to get to Vamist's house by tomorrow night if you ate any of it."

Killer looked at Morwen. "You mean it would slow me down? I thought you said it made those plants safe!"

"Safe to walk near, not safe to eat." Morwen knelt next to the chokevines and began to dig. "And I don't know whether you'd slow down or not. So far, you haven't reacted with any particular consistency to any of the things you've eaten."

"It's possible that the slowstone would inhibit the onset of any alteration resulting from the consumption of invisible dusk-blooming chokevines," Telemain said. "There is precedent for such an eventuality in Killer's response to the growth-enhancing qualities of MacDonald's fertilizer, although the parallel is not perfect."

"What did he say?" Killer asked anxiously.

"That the slowstone might slow down your reaction to the invisible dusk-blooming chokevines, instead of slowing *you* down." Having dug all the way around the roots of both plants, Morwen slid her trowel under the clump of dirt and carefully lifted the first paralyzed chokevine into a sample bag. "Unfortunately, the only way to tell for certain would be to try it and see what happens."

"You mean the vines might do something to me, too, if I ate them? Why didn't you warn me?"

"I did."

"You told me they were dangerous! You didn't say they were magical."

Trouble gave Killer a look of deep disgust. "You think normal plants get named *invisible* dusk-blooming chokevines?"

"But they aren't invisible!" Killer protested. "Not to me."

"Then maybe nothing would happen to you if you ate one," Cimorene said. "You can experiment later. Morwen, are you finished? We've been longer than five minutes, and I'd like to get going again."

"I'm done." Climbing to her feet, Morwen tucked the sample bags and trowel into her sleeve and smiled. "And I believe I've thought of a way to speed up the rest of the trip. Have you got any rope in your pack?"

18

In Which They Concoct a Plan

Cimorene looked at Morwen, frowning. "Rope? I think so. Why?"

"So we can tow Killer," Morwen said. "Between the laundry basket and the broomstick, we should have plenty of power, and we'll be able to go a lot faster, now that we're out of the trees."

"Good idea," Brandel said. "It's a pity you didn't think of it sooner. I've got plenty of rope back at the tower."

"I don't know about this," Killer said. "It doesn't sound very comfortable."

"Do you want to run all the way to Vamist's house?" Morwen said. "That's your other choice. Take it or leave it."

Killer took it, but not without grumbling the whole

time they spent rigging a harness for him and tying it to the laundry basket and broomstick.

"This is undignified," he complained as they prepared to start off once more.

"What's so dignified about a six-foot floating blue donkey with oversized wings?" said Scorn.

"I'm very . . . very . . . Eee-augh! Help! Slow down! Oh, I knew this was a bad idea. Rabbits weren't meant to go this fast."

Morwen glanced back and almost laughed. Killer hung at the end of the tow ropes, all four feet braced against the air (which did him no good whatsoever). His wings and ears streamed behind him in the wind. On his back, barely visible between the blue ears and feathers, Scorn and Horatio lay flat with their front claws dug into the rope harness.

Smiling, Morwen turned back to concentrate on flying the broomstick. Despite Killer's loud complaints, by her standards they were not traveling particularly fast. Between the extra weight on both broom and basket and the energy it took to pull Killer, Morwen estimated their speed at about a third of her usual rate. Still, it was much faster than walking, especially over the open meadows that stretched ahead of them.

They had gone several miles and Killer's objections had degenerated into occasional terrified brays when Brandel slowed the laundry basket. Morwen matched his reduction in speed, and a moment later they landed in a small stand of trees near the top of a hill.

"That's enough of that!" Killer said. "I don't care if you want to get there quickly, I don't care if I have to run, I don't care if those wizards turn me into a pancake and eat me for breakfast. I'm *not* doing that again."

"You won't have to," Brandel said, climbing out of the laundry basket. "Vamist's house is over this hill and down the road about a quarter of a mile." He looked at Cimorene a little apologetically. "I know you'd rather be closer, but with him making all that noise—"

"You'd make noise, too, if you were being hauled along three times as fast as any reasonable rabbit should go," Killer said unrepentantly.

"Well, you're not being pulled anywhere now, so be quiet," Cimorene said. "If you do anything that messes up our getting Mendanbar's sword, I'll . . . I'll turn you into a pancake and eat you myself."

"You can't do that!" Killer's ears jerked nervously. "Can you?"

"I can try."

"Killer will behave himself." Morwen looked at her cats. "Scorn and Trouble will see to it." And between keeping Killer out of mischief and acting as lookouts, the cats might actually have so much to do that *they* wouldn't get up to anything unfortunate. She hoped.

Cimorene nodded and turned to Brandel. "How easy will it be to sneak up on this house without being seen?"

"It shouldn't be too difficult," Brandel replied. "There are a lot of trees and bushes around the house."

"Let's go, then."

"What about these?" Brandel asked, waving at the empty laundry basket and broomstick.

"Leave the basket here," Morwen said. "It's too

awkward to carry, and I can always enchant another one for you when this is all over. I'll take the broomstick in case Cimorene and I need to get away quickly."

"Then we're ready," Cimorene said. "Let's *go*."

Twisting his rings absently, Telemain nodded and started up the hill. The rest followed in silence. No one seemed to feel much like talking as they went up over the hill and down the tree-lined lane on the other side.

A few minutes later, Brandel stopped and looked at Cimorene. "Vamist's house is just around the bend. If you and Morwen cut through these bushes and head off to the right, you should come out in his backyard."

"Good," said Morwen. "Scorn, Trouble, run ahead and find out which room the sword is in and where Antorell and Vamist are. Don't forget to come back and let me know."

"We aren't *amateurs*," Scorn said, switching her tail.

"Right," said Trouble. "And Kazul's not here, so I get first crack at the wizard." He stood up and stretched to show that it wasn't all that important, then vanished into the bushes.

"I don't know why you care so much about the wizard," Scorn said, following. "That obnoxious idiot with no hair is the one I want dibs on. The things he said . . ."

Frowning, Morwen looked after the cats. "When we get back I'm going to have to make one of them tell me just what Arona Michaelear Grinogion Vamist said when he called the other day. Scorn is really annoyed."

"Yow mrow," said Horatio, and began washing his left front paw.

A few minutes later, the two cats returned. "Vamist and Antorell are in a big room with glass doors at the side of the house," Trouble reported. "They've got the sword on the table and they're arguing."

"Arguing?" said Morwen.

"About what to do with the sword. Vamist thinks the Society of Wizards should stick it into a rock and leave it somewhere because that's traditional, but Antorell says that's only for important swords that are supposed to be found again. I don't think he knows what that sword does."

"Or else he doesn't want it found," said Scorn.

"Hmph. We'll see about that." Morwen turned to the others. "Trouble says things haven't changed much since we saw them in the mirror. Cimorene and I will leave now; Killer, you come with us." She looked at Telemain. "You two get ready, and I'll send Scorn to signal you when to knock on the door."

"Good luck," Telemain said, and the two groups started off in different directions.

Sneaking up on Arona Michaelear Grinogion Vamist's house was much easier than Morwen had expected. The garden at the rear of the house was wildly overgrown, so there were plenty of shrubs to hide behind, and most of the windows were covered with dense vines. As far as Morwen could tell, all anyone would be able to see out of those windows were the back sides of leaves.

As they approached, Scorn vanished under a scraggly chrysanthemum. She returned a moment later. "They're still arguing. The doors are over here on the left."

Morwen translated for Cimorene, who nodded and

murmured, "Good. Killer, you stay here. And don't eat anything. Arona Vamist consorts with wizards, so there's no telling what he has in his garden."

Weeds, mostly. It looks as if he hasn't paid attention to it for years, Morwen thought, but this was no time to say so. She looked at Scorn and said softly, "As soon as we're next to the doors, go around to the front so Telemain and Brandel will know when to knock."

"No problem," said Scorn.

"And don't forget to come back when they've seen you," Trouble said. "You don't want to get left behind."

Scorn looked at him. "I won't be left behind. Telemain's the one who's doing the transport spell."

"Enough," said Morwen. "Do your jobs and argue about it later." She started toward the corner of the house.

"Are you going to be long?" said Killer.

"Keep your voice down," Cimorene whispered. "I don't know, so stay alert. We're going to be leaving in something of a hurry."

Trouble snorted. "There's an understatement."

Cautiously, they edged up to the corner, leaving Killer to watch anxiously from among the vines. Long ago, someone had built a stone patio along the far side of the house, with a flower border along the south edge and a row of tall bushes to the west for privacy. Now, weeds and grass grew in the cracks between stones, the bushes were an untidy mass of prickly twigs, and the flower border was full of thistles. Cimorene and Morwen had to step carefully to avoid being stuck.

Scorn directed them to a spot that was in easy reach of the glass doors but still out of sight. As soon as they were in position, Trouble insinuated himself between the vines and the wall of the house and crept around the corner and out of sight.

"He's ready," said Scorn after a minute. "See you later." She threw Morwen a slow blink of affection and disappeared into the unpruned hedge.

The wait that followed seemed to last hours. Morwen could feel Cimorene's tension, and she was not exactly calm herself. Planning to avoid a direct confrontation with any wizard—even if it was only Antorell—was all very well, but there was no guarantee that the wizard would cooperate. She fingered her sleeves, wishing that witches' spells did not take such a long time to perform, or that there were some way of storing them for quick use, the way wizards did.

The ivy trembled, and an instant later Trouble appeared. "They've left the room. Both of them. And the sword is just sitting on the table."

"Did you spot any alarm spells?" Morwen asked.

"Nope." Trouble lashed his tail.

"This sounds too easy." But Morwen turned to Cimorene anyway and said, "They're gone."

"Then let's go." Cimorene stepped over a patch of gigantic dandelions onto the ruined patio, and Morwen followed. Together they crossed to a set of double doors made of small rectangular windowpanes, eight down and four across on each door.

Cautiously, Morwen tried the handle. With a sharp click, the latch opened and the right-hand door popped half an inch inward.

They looked at each other, and without a word they leaned forward to peer through the nearest windowpane. The room looked just as empty of people as

Trouble had claimed, though it was rather full of other things. Ornate chairs lined the walls, and most of them had things piled on their seats. One held a stack of books; another, a clay pot filled with dirt; a third, a stuffed pigeon sitting on a stringless violin. Two dusty suits of armor holding spears stood on either side of the far door, and the walls were covered with cobwebby pictures. In the center of the room was a large table, with two chairs pulled out crookedly from opposite sides, as if the occupants had gotten up quickly.

In the center of the table, shiny and positively reeking of magic, lay an unsheathed sword.

Cimorene looked at Morwen and sighed. "It must be a trap. But that's Mendanbar's sword in there, for certain, and we have to try to get it. And I don't think we're going to have much time. Any suggestions?"

"Quit fussing and go get the silly thing," Trouble said.

"Are you volunteering to be first in line?" Morwen asked.

"Why not?" Trouble rose on his back legs and set his front paws against the unlatched door. As it swung inward, he dropped to all fours once more and sauntered through. He paused just out of reach, glanced around, and then took a short running start and leapt onto the table. Looking very smug, he twitched his tail and sat down on the hilt of the sword.

"I should have known better," Morwen muttered. "Well, at least we know he was right about the alarms. If there were any, that performance would have set them off."

"Then let's—"

From the front of the building came a loud, angry

yowl, carrying easily over and around the intervening walls. Trouble jumped to attention, straddling the sword, and Morwen took a worried half step toward the sound before she caught herself. *The sword is the important thing right now,* she reminded herself, but she couldn't quite make herself believe it.

"That's torn it." Shoving the door the rest of the way open, Cimorene darted inside. Morwen had no real choice except to follow.

"Drat," she said, and did so.

As Cimorene ran across the two yards of open space that separated the doors and the table, Morwen felt a ripple of magic in the air. "Cimorene, stop!" she said, but she was not quite in time. The ripple hit Cimorene and froze her motionless, one hand stiffly extended toward the hilt of Mendanbar's sword.

"Oh!" said Cimorene. "I can't move. Morwen, what's happened? Can you do something about it?"

"*I* am what has happened!" said a new voice, and one of the suits of armor shifted and began to change. Its hard edges blurred and darkened, and its feet and legs spread out into a long robe. The spear it held lost its head and shrank a foot and a half. Last of all, the face came clear.

"Antorell!" said Cimorene.

"Exactly," the wizard said with an evil grin. "And I don't think there's anything at all that your witchy friend can do about me."

Morwen's eyes narrowed. "We'll see about that." She pointed at him and said firmly, "Argelfraster."

Nothing happened.

19

In Which They Confront the Villains

A startled expression crossed Antorell's face. Then he smiled smugly and said, "You see? I have taken care of your little spell."

Hmph, thought Morwen. *I certainly don't believe* that. *He's probably just out of range. Now, how can I get close enough to melt him before he gets suspicious and freezes me?*

"How interesting that Mendanbar sent the two of you to retrieve this"—Antorell waved his free hand at the sword, and Trouble bristled—"instead of coming himself. It must not be as important to him as Father thought it was. Not that it matters now. Even if Father and the others haven't taken control of the castle yet—"

"Taken control of the castle?" Cimorene sounded

thoroughly alarmed. "I *knew* there was something wrong at home."

"And just how was the Society of Wizards planning to take over the castle of the King of the Enchanted Forest?" Morwen asked in as politely skeptical a tone as she could manage.

Antorell flushed angrily. "One man is no match for the combined might of the Society of Wizards."

"He has been until now," Morwen said. *Of course, until now he's had the sword. It's a good thing Cimorene sent Kazul back last night; it sounds as if Mendanbar can use the help.*

"Until now, we have not acted in concert," Antorell said. "But yesterday morning, all of the wizards of the Society of Wizards, led by my father, the Head Wizard Zemenar, transported themselves to the Enchanted Forest to take the magic that rightfully belongs to us. By this time, they should be finishing up their work."

"Yesterday morning?" Morwen blinked. "So that's what disrupted Telemain's transportation spell! He must have gotten caught in the backwash of the Society of Wizards transporting *en masse*."

"Mendanbar and Kazul are quite capable of handling your society between them," Cimorene said to Antorell, putting up her chin.

The wizard frowned. "I doubt that. Father is prepared for anything."

"It's hard to be prepared for the King of the Dragons."

Antorell seemed to have forgotten Morwen for the moment. Hoping to move close enough for the melting spell to work, she stepped sideways around the end of the table. Unfortunately, the movement attracted his attention.

"Halt!" Antorell raised his staff and pointed it at her. "Stay where you are, or I'll see to it that you can't move, either."

"Try it," Trouble growled. "Just try it."

Muffled noises filtered through the door beside Antorell. A moment later, it swung open. Antorell glanced over and moved away as Telemain entered, supporting Brandel with one arm. Brandel's face was a grayish white, and his eyes were glassy. Even across the room, Morwen could smell a burned odor.

Telemain's eyes met hers. "He lost his temper, and the reflective sidewash from the shielding enchantment on Vamist produced a temporary circulating phase inversion at the energy source. He'll be all right in a few minutes."

"His own magic bounced back and stunned him," Morwen translated for Cimorene's benefit. Then she looked past Telemain and stiffened. Behind Telemain and Brandel, the bald, sharp-faced man they had seen in the mirror entered, carrying Scorn at arm's length by the scruff of her neck. He had reason for caution: his hands were covered with scratches. Scorn's eyes were narrowed to slits and she was panting for breath, but she still managed an occasional swipe with a paw. Unfortunately, she wasn't close enough to the bald man to connect.

"Put that cat down immediately," Morwen said. "You're suffocating her. Adult cats aren't meant to be carried that way."

"Oh, is it yours?" said the bald man. "You should train it better. It's not very well behaved."

Trouble bunched himself together and growled. If Telemain and Brandel had not been between him and Scorn's captor, Morwen thought, he would have leapt to the rescue at once.

"You seem to have had some difficulty after all, Vamist," said Antorell to the bald man. "I did warn you."

"It was nothing I couldn't handle," said Vamist.

"Put that cat *down*," Morwen repeated, sliding her hands into her sleeves in search of something to throw.

"You'd better do it," Cimorene said. "Hurting one of her cats is the only thing I know of that makes Morwen lose her temper."

"Morwen!" Vamist's eyes widened, and he brandished Scorn as if she were a banner. "The so-called witch? Then you should thank me for—ow!"

Suddenly, Vamist jumped and flailed his arms in a desperate attempt to keep his balance. Morwen glimpsed a black-and-white blur between his feet. Then Trouble launched himself from the table, ricocheted off Brandel's shoulder, and landed, claws extended, on top of Vamist's bald head. Vamist howled and dropped Scorn, who landed heavily and dragged herself under the table, wheezing audibly. As he grabbed at Trouble, Morwen pulled the collapsible bucket from her sleeve and threw it.

The bucket hit Vamist in the shoulder just as he got a grip on one of Trouble's legs. The impact wasn't heavy enough to do any real damage, but it startled him into losing his hold. Trouble took a final swipe at the back of Vamist's neck and dropped to the floor, where he joined Horatio under a chair.

"You little—" Vamist bent and grabbed at the cats, only to trip over Telemain's conveniently extended foot. He went sprawling, and Telemain smiled slightly.

"You all right, Scorn?" Trouble asked, his voice slightly muffled by the table and chairs.

"I will be in a minute," Scorn said. She sounded hoarse but angry. "Save some of that creep for me."

"Grrrow," said Horatio, and he wound between the chair legs to Scorn's side, where he began washing her neck.

"Nothing you can't handle, eh, Vamist?" said Antorell. "No wonder you needed our help. You did fine as long as all you had to deal with were ordinary townspeople, but you can't handle even one witch's cats."

"I don't—yowch!" When Vamist looked up to answer Antorell, Horatio had reached out and calmly dug his claws into Vamist's hand. Vamist pulled back out of reach, glared at Horatio, and said, "*Traditional* witches have *one* black cat. These are clearly not proper witches' cats, and there are far too many of them. Had we had the opportunity to discuss it, I would have advised that witch to dispose of these—these mongrels and find a more suitable companion."

"Is *that* what you called about?" Morwen said. "No wonder the cats were furious!"

"Do you blame us?" said Trouble. " 'Dispose of these mongrels,' indeed!"

"I can see how successful your persuasion would have been," Antorell said to Vamist.

"There are always those who insist on ignoring the

great traditions," Vamist said with an attempt at dignity. "They are foredoomed to failure."

"Of course. You're doing this"—Antorell waved at the sword—"out of the goodness of your heart. You don't need us to protect you from the fire-witches, because they're doomed to failure. Right?"

"You're as bad as he is," Brandel said, scowling at the wizard. He still leaned heavily on Telemain, but his color was improving rapidly and his eyes had lost their glassy look.

For the first time, Antorell took a good look at Brandel. "A fire-witch! How fortunate. My staff can use a little more magic, and yours will do very nicely." Antorell stepped forward and raised his staff.

Morwen's lips tightened. She was no closer to Antorell than she had been, so she still couldn't make Telemain's melting spell work. Telemain was near enough, but he was very sensibly saving what was left of his magic for the transportation spell that would take them all back to the Enchanted Forest. Brandel didn't know the melting spell, and Cimorene was close enough but couldn't move to point her finger because of Antorell's spell. *Antorell's spell—wizard's magic. Mendanbar's sword automatically counters wizard's magic. The sword . . .*

Morwen leaned forward and grabbed the hilt of Mendanbar's sword. It felt as if she had grabbed the hot end of a poker, but she hung on. *Only for a minute, only long enough to swing it,* she thought, and swept the flat of the blade up against Cimorene's arm. A jolt of magic shook her hand loose as the sword absorbed the wizard's spell, and the blade clattered to the table. At exactly the same instant, Antorell's staff exploded.

Everyone ducked, including Cimorene. "Ow! My staff!" yelled Antorell. "This isn't poss—Cimorene!"

Cimorene pointed at him. "Argelfraster. Argelfraster, you nasty little thief."

Antorell began to melt. "Noooo! Cimorene, this is all your fault. I spent months making that staff! I'll get you for this, I swear I will. If it takes me twenty years, I'll get you. You'll be sorry. You'll be . . ." His voice trailed off into a gurgle. Arona Vamist leaned forward, staring incredulously at Antorell's empty robe and the spreading puddle of brown goo on his floor.

"Well, that takes care of *him*," Cimorene said with considerable satisfaction. "Who blew up his staff?"

"I think it was Mendanbar's sword," Morwen said, gesturing.

"No," said Telemain with utter certainty. "The sword was not responsible. I was observing with great care, and the necessary connections for such a serious shift interference were not present."

"Then who did it?" Brandel asked.

"I suspect you did." Telemain let go of Brandel, waited a moment to make sure the fire-witch would not fall over, and then began picking up splinters of Antorell's staff. "At this point, it is only speculation, but a fundamental incompatibility between your magic and that of a wizard would account for the phenomenon very nicely. I will be able to say for certain after I do a few tests."

"Good," said Cimorene. "Do them after we get back." Gingerly, she leaned forward and picked up Mendanbar's sword. Morwen's hand still felt sore and she could not help flinching, but although Cimorene held it with obvious care, the sword did not appear to bother her. "And now that we've got this, we can—"

"Not so fast!" Arona Michaelear Grinogion Vamist had straightened and edged around the table as Antorell melted. Now he picked up a clay pot filled with dirt from the seat of a nearby chair and held it poised to throw. The angry red scratches that covered his hands and head made him look very fierce. "Put that sword down at once and leave."

"No," said Cimorene. "It's my husband's sword, and I'm taking it home. Telemain, how soon can you do that transportation spell?"

"The initial preparations require a mental effort that—" Telemain paused, looked at Cimorene, and then said carefully, "I'll be ready in a minute or two."

"Thank you," Cimorene said, smiling. "Then let's—"

"Cimorene, duck!"

Cimorene dodged in response to Morwen's shout, and Arona Vamist's clay pot flew over her left shoulder. For a moment, it looked like a clean miss. Then Cimorene yelled in surprise and clawed at her face with her free hand. Even before Morwen saw the pot dangling from nothing at all down Cimorene's back, she knew.

"It's an invisible dusk-blooming chokevine," she said. "Stay back, everyone, or it'll grab you, too."

"I warned you," Vamist said. "*Now* will you leave?"

"Get that thing off Cimorene."

"No. Not until you leave."

"I bet he doesn't know how," Trouble said.

"He kept it from attacking him when he threw it," Scorn objected. "He must know *something*."

"Well, why don't you shove him into it and see what happens?" Trouble emerged from underneath the table and approached Vamist.

"Good idea." Morwen stalked around the table to join Trouble.

"What's a good idea?" Vamist said, backing away from them along the far side of the table. "You get out of my house, all of you!"

"Aren't you finished yet?" said Killer from the doorway. "I thought this wasn't supposed to take long."

"What is *that?*" said Vamist, looking wildly over his shoulder.

"Killer!" said Morwen. "Get in here and eat this vine immediately."

"Isn't that one of those things you say you can't see?" Killer said doubtfully, shoving his way through the partly open double doors. "You said before that they weren't safe. And what if there are side effects?"

"Eat it!" Morwen said. "I'll take care of the side effects later. Hurry up!" Cimorene had kept her grip on the sword and she was still on her feet, but she was beginning to turn blue.

"If you say so." Killer stretched out his neck and bit at the air in back of Cimorene. The clay pot crashed to the floor and shattered, spewing dirt and shards of clay, while Killer munched thoughtfully. "Not bad. It's much more delicate than I'd expected from the way it smells, though. And I can't quite place the flavor." He nibbled delicately next to Cimorene's ear.

Cimorene choked, gasped, and began to regain her proper color. Taking two or three deep breaths, she made a series of brushing and pulling motions around her head and shoulders.

"Hey!" said Killer. "You're knocking it all over the floor!"

Cimorene coughed and glared at him. "That's the idea."

"But it'll get all dusty!"

"You won't have time to worry about that," Vamist said. "I have other snares in my house for criminals and thieves!"

Dodging between two chairs, he jabbed his thumb against a wooden flower carved into the wall. With a high-pitched screeching of metal against metal, the suit of armor next to the door raised its spear to throw.

"Telemain," cried Morwen, "get us out of here!"

The suit of armor let fly. Cimorene evaded the missile easily, but Killer was too large to avoid it quickly. As the edges of the room blurred and ran together in the beginning of Telemain's transportation spell, the spear struck the left side of Killer's chest.

"Eeee-augh!"

Killer reared back, wings flapping. As the mist of transportation cleared, he sat down on the air six inches above a clump of violets. The spear fell to the ground below him with a loud thump, flattening a strip of moss.

"Killer!" said Cimorene. "Oh no! Morwen—"

With the back of her mind, Morwen noted that Telemain had managed to transport them all the way back to the Enchanted Forest in one jump, and that for some reason he had brought Arona Michaelear Grinogion Vamist along. Most of her attention, however, was centered on Killer, who was flopping around in a manner that would have looked exceptionally silly if she had not been so concerned.

"Stop floundering about like that," Morwen said to the donkey. "I can't do anything to help if I can't get near you."

"Waugh!" Killer rolled sideways and struggled to his feet. "That was uncomfortable. Am I dead?"

"No such luck," said Scorn.

Everyone stared at Killer. There was not a mark on him to show where the spear had struck, though they had all seen it hit him. Then Trouble sauntered forward. Reaching up, he batted at Killer's front hooves. His paw went right through them as if there were nothing in the way but air.

"That's a handy trick," Trouble said. "How'd you do it?"

"Do what?" Killer asked. He looked down in time to see Trouble jump through his right leg. "Eee-augh! I'm a ghost! Oh, help."

"You can't be a ghost," Cimorene said. "It's the middle of the day. Ghosts only come out at night."

"Most of them," Morwen corrected. "I knew a ghost once who was afraid of the dark, so he always appeared at noon. He had a terrible time scaring anyone. Still, I believe you're right about Killer."

"If I'm not a ghost, why is that—that *cat* prancing through me like this?" Killer demanded.

"Side effect," said Morwen. "An extremely opportune side effect, in fact. Eating that invisible dusk-blooming chokevine seems to have made you insubstantial."

"Shouldn't it have made him invisible?" Brandel asked.

"Not necessarily," Telemain said. "The pattern of interactivity among the various layers of enchantment affecting Killer is such that the precise effect of additional incidents is not subject to the usual predictive methods."

"Eeeeee-aaauugh!" Killer's wail of distress was louder and longer than any of his earlier complaints. "If I'm insubstantial, how am I going to *eat?*"

"We'll take care of that as soon as we return Mendanbar's sword," Morwen told him. "Telemain, if you're quite recovered, we should—Arona Michaelear Grinogion Vamist! Where do you think you're going?"

"Somewhere else," Vamist said. "You have no right to kidnap me like this."

"And *you* have no business aiding and abetting the theft of important magical items from the King of the Enchanted Forest," Cimorene said.

"Besides, I'm a witch," Morwen put in. "Isn't it *traditional* for witches to steal people away?"

"Not people like me!" Vamist said. "Babies and princesses."

"Babies and princesses are of no practical use whatsoever," Morwen said. "Most of them, anyway. And the ones that are useful don't need to be kidnapped."

"That's not the point!"

"No," said Cimorene. "The point is that we have more important things to do right now. We'll deal with you later; until then, you stay with us. Telemain, can you take us to the castle now?"

"It will be simpler if you will all stand a little closer

together," Telemain said. "That's better." He gestured, and the familiar mist rose around them.

When it cleared, they found themselves in a large empty area. Forty feet ahead of them, the enormous trees of the Enchanted Forest rose in massive splendor, but where they stood were only ashes and bare, blackened ground. For a moment, Morwen thought Telemain had made a mistake. Then she turned her head and saw the castle, with its improbable towers and windows and staircases, shimmering inside a giant ball of golden light.

"Good heavens!" said Cimorene, speaking for them all. "What's *happened?*"

20

In Which Disaster Strikes

For a long moment, no one answered. Then Morwen said, in a voice that sounded grim even to herself, "The Society of Wizards happened. I just wonder where they've all disappeared to."

"Good riddance, wherever it is," Scorn said. "*What* a mess."

"Maybe they're inside the castle?" Brandel suggested.

"No," said a pleasant female voice behind them. "Outside the forest. At least, that's what the dragons tell us. Hello, Brandel; it's nice to see you again."

"Amory!" Brandel spun around, kicking up a small cloud of ash, and hugged the slender red-haired woman standing in back of him. "So Marli passed my message on."

"Yes, and we've certainly had an interesting time of it." The red-haired woman smiled over Brandel's shoulder at the rest of the group. "I'm Brandel's cousin Amory. You must be Queen Cimorene and the others King Kazul told us about. She wants to see you right away."

"I should hope so," said Trouble.

"What's been going on here?" asked Cimorene. "And where's Mendanbar?"

"Who?" said Amory.

"The King of the Enchanted Forest," Brandel said. "Her husband."

"Oh. I'm afraid I don't know anything about him. I think King Kazul does, though."

"Then take us to Kazul right away," Cimorene said.

Telemain took hold of Vamist's shoulder—the bald man had been trying to slip off again, although there was nowhere near to slip off to—and they followed Amory around the castle. As they walked, little eddies of ash followed everyone except Killer. The cats were very unhappy about the way the fine gray particles stuck to them; Trouble even tried to jump onto Killer's back to get out of the dust, having forgotten about the donkey's lack of solidity.

A quarter of the way around the castle, they saw the first few dragons walking purposefully along the boundary between the forest and the ashy area. As they went on, they saw more dragons, some walking, some flying above the trees. A number of red-haired people—presumably more of Brandel's fire-witch relatives—were standing guard near the edge of the glow that surrounded the castle. Amory nodded to them in passing and cut across the open area to the forest on the far side.

Kazul was just inside the forest, talking with another dragon and two more fire-witches.

". . . and now it seems to have stopped growing completely, Your Majesty." The second dragon had a deep, clear voice that carried plainly to the approaching party. "Nobody's sure why."

"Well, it's a good thing, whatever the reason," Kazul said. "Send someone over to—"

"Kazul!" Cimorene quickened her pace. "What's been happening? Where's Mendanbar?"

"I think he's still in there," Kazul said, nodding at the castle, which was partially visible through the trees. "I see you got the sword. I'm glad *something's* gone right lately."

Trouble and Scorn ran ahead and jumped onto Kazul's tail, but Horatio hung back.

"Mrow?"

"If Kazul doesn't care, I don't see why you should," Scorn told him, and began to wash the ashes off of her back.

"You *think* Mendanbar's in the castle?" Cimorene paled slightly. "Why don't you know? Kazul—"

"Stop flapping your wings over it and let the dust settle," Kazul said. "I'll explain in a minute. Marchak, send someone to notify the air patrol about this area, and tell them that if they find any other ashed-out spots they're to check whether the spots are stable before they report in. Let them know that Cimorene's back, with Mendanbar's sword."

"Right away, Your Majesty," said the other dragon. With a cheerful wave in Cimorene's direction, he walked off.

Cimorene took a deep breath. "Kazul, tell me right away. Is Mendanbar all right, or . . . or . . ."

"Mendanbar is *not* dead," Morwen said firmly.

"Why are you so sure of that?" Kazul asked.

"I've lived in the Enchanted Forest for a long time. I was here four years ago when the old King, Mendanbar's father, died. Believe me, when a King of the Enchanted Forest dies, the forest makes sure everyone knows it. I didn't get a good night's sleep for a week, and neither did anyone else."

Trouble looked up from washing his tail. "*Including* cats," he said in tones of deep disapproval. "I remember that."

"That's good," Kazul said. Then her head turned to look at the castle and the sphere of gold light that surrounded it. "I think." She glanced at Cimorene and sighed. "It was the Society of Wizards."

"*Of course* it was the Society of Wizards," Cimorene said shortly, and Killer backed away from her, ears twitching nervously. "But what, exactly, did they *do?*"

"Well, when I got here late last night, they had the castle surrounded," Kazul said. "They must have been using their staffs a lot, because there was a good thirty yards of dead forest around the castle already. I thought it would be better to head back to the Mountains of Morning for reinforcements."

"I should think so!" said Amory. "Even a dragon can't take on the whole Society of Wizards single-handed. 'Scuse me, Your Majesty."

"We attacked at dawn," Kazul continued. "About

fifteen minutes after the fight started, that bubble went up around the castle and no one could get in. A couple of wizards came out, but I'm afraid they, ah, got eaten in all the excitement, and no one thought to ask them any questions first. So we don't know what happened inside."

"Isn't there some way of finding out?" Cimorene turned to Telemain. "Can't you adjust your magic mirror spell to get through that bubble, now that you know it's there? If I could talk to somebody inside—"

"There isn't anybody inside, Your Majesty," said a new voice, and everyone turned to see Willin, the castle steward, standing by the base of a nearby oak. The normally immaculate elf looked awful: his gold lace collar was torn and blackened; his crisp white shirt was wrinkled, dusty, and smeared with ashes; his velvet coat was ripped in several places and was missing most of its buttons; his white silk hose were torn and dirty; and his left shoe had lost its gold heel.

"Willin!" said Cimorene. "Sit down—you look exhausted. What happened? How do you know there's no one in the castle?"

"I should say, no one other than His Majesty," Willin said. "When he realized that the Society of Wizards intended to attack the castle, he sent the staff away. Including me. I wouldn't have left, Your Majesty, only he insisted . . ."

"You mean Mendanbar was all alone in there when the wizards got here?"

"An unusual strategy, but quite possibly an extremely effective one," Telemain said thoughtfully. "I doubt that anyone but Mendanbar really knows all the passages in that castle, and with everyone else gone, he could use his magic full force, without worrying about hurting someone on his own side."

"Well, it doesn't seem to have worked very well, does it?" Cimorene snapped.

"Kazul, did you manage to catch Head Wizard Zemenar?" Morwen asked. "If anyone knows what the Society of Wizards did, he does."

Kazul shifted in evident embarrassment. "I'm afraid I ate Zemenar myself. I caught up with him coming out of the Caves of Chance just a little while ago, and by then I was so angry . . ."

"It's a good thing you did," Amory put in. "That was what set the rest of them running. Before then, we were barely holding our own."

"I'm confused," Killer said. "And this talk about eating is making me hungry. Somebody explain it all so we can have lunch."

"You can't have lunch," Trouble said. "You're insubstantial."

"So somebody can fix me, and *then* we can have lunch," Killer said.

"I'm confused, too," Brandel said. "Even if I'm not particularly hungry."

"Then let us take things in a proper order," said Telemain, for all the world as if he were talking about laying out a new spell. "Willin, you are the reasonable person to begin. What happened at the castle after we left?"

Willin glanced at Cimorene to make sure it was all right to let this unofficial person take charge. When she nodded, he began to speak. At first, the others interrupted him frequently with questions, but Telemain insisted that answers wait until the whole tale had been told. Once they realized that he meant it, everyone except the cats stopped interrupting.

The first wizards, Willin said, had turned up almost as soon as Cimorene and her party had left the Enchanted Forest. Mendanbar had melted them with Telemain's spell, but they had damaged several sections of the Enchanted Forest before he caught up with them. Without the sword, he could not repair the harm they'd done, and he had been very concerned. To help minimize the problem, he'd called in several tribes of elves and asked them to keep watch.

"The elves could melt some of the wizards with soapy water and lemon juice," Willin said, "and if they couldn't get close enough, or if there were too many wizards, they could let the King know right away. Then he'd come and take care of the wizards before they did too much damage."

Unfortunately, the wizards were well prepared. The following morning, the entire Society of Wizards had appeared outside the castle. Before anyone had realized what was happening, they had destroyed a wide patch of the forest, leaving the elves no way of getting near them with buckets of soapy water.

"That was when King Mendanbar sent us away," Willin finished sadly. "I tried to make him let me stay, I really did, but—"

"I understand," Cimorene said. "You did your best."

"Did you see what happened outside the castle after you left?" Telemain asked.

"Some of it. The wizards cleared a twenty-foot ring around the castle and then spent most of the day working some spell; I wasn't close enough to see what.

Around the middle of the afternoon, the circle they'd cleared started to expand. Fortunately, it didn't grow very fast, and those of us who were watching had plenty of time to move back. Then about ten of them walked across the main bridge into the castle. That's all I can tell you, I'm afraid. It got harder to see what was going on because I kept having to move back to stay out of sight."

"Was Head Wizard Zemenar one of the group that went into the castle?" Morwen asked.

Willin nodded.

Turning to Kazul, Telemain said, "So when you got here that night, Zemenar was inside the castle and the rest of the Society of Wizards were camped in the burned-out area just outside."

"Right," said Kazul. "I called in the rest of my people, and we attacked in the morning. Four or five wizards came out of the castle, the shield spell went up—"

"Wait a minute," said Brandel. "Shield spell?"

"That glow around the castle," said Telemain. "The Society of Wizards invented it, and it's really a remarkable piece of work. Nobody can get in or out while it's up, not even a dragon—remember, Morwen?—and they're the only people who can take it down."

"Not quite," Morwen said. "Mendanbar's sword got rid of the last one we ran into."

"Mmmm, yes. Cimorene, how well can you use that sword?"

"I can't use it at all really, the way you mean," Cimorene replied. "From what Mendanbar said, the sword has to . . . to agree to work for you somehow before you can use it for magic, and it'll only do that for the Kings of the Enchanted Forest and their direct descendants. I'm a member of the family, so it will let me hold it as a sort of courtesy, but I'm not a direct descendant of any of the Kings of the Enchanted Forest, so I can't use its magic."

"Blast. It's probably got a selectivity module in the central linkage generator, and if it's braided to the spell core . . ." Telemain's voice trailed off into muttering.

Morwen frowned. The last time they had encountered the Society of Wizards' shield spell, the wizards had been using it to hold Kazul prisoner. And if she remembered correctly . . . She caught Trouble's eye and motioned to him. Tilting his head, Trouble considered for a moment. Then he jumped down from Kazul's back and sauntered over.

"What is it?"

"Do you think you could get inside the shield spell around the castle?" Morwen asked in a low voice. If the answer was no, she didn't want Cimorene getting her hopes up.

"I don't see why not," Trouble said. "Jasper did it last time, and I'm as good at that sort of thing as he is."

Morwen didn't bother to ask what sort of thing he was talking about. If it was a cat sort of thing, as was likely, Trouble wouldn't explain anyway, and questioning him might make him refuse to help at all. "I'd like you to go inside and see if you can find out what's happened to Mendanbar."

Trouble's ears pricked up in interest. "Sounds amusing," he said in a tone that tried to be casual and failed. "I'll do it."

As he walked off toward the castle, Morwen hid a smile. Now that he'd realized he could get inside, it would take more than wizards to keep him from satisfying his curiosity. She turned her attention back to the main conversation as Amory said, ". . . doing very well when we got here."

Kazul snorted. "You're being generous. We weren't doing well at all." She looked at Cimorene. "It's hard to fight when you're having an allergy attack, and with all those wizards' staffs in one place every dragon for miles was sneezing so hard they could barely see straight."

"I understand perfectly," Cimorene said. "And thank you both for trying."

Kazul must have heard something in her tone that everyone else missed, because she lowered her head almost to the ground so she could look at Cimorene eye to eye and said, "It will be all right, Cimorene. If he's not dead—and if Morwen says we'd know, then we'd know—then he's probably perfectly all right. All we have to do is get him out of the castle."

"And how are we going to do that?" Cimorene said crossly. "The sword is the only thing that can get rid of that shield, and he's the only one who can use the sword."

"We'll think of something," Kazul said.

"In the meantime, what are you going to do about *him?*" Brandel asked with a dark look in Vamist's direction.

"If he's a wizard, I'm sure I can find someone to eat him once you're finished with him," Kazul offered. "*Everyone* can't be full yet."

Vamist turned white, making the cat scratches on

his head look even redder. "You can't do this to me!"

"Why not?" Morwen said. "It's *traditional* for dragons to eat people, isn't it?"

"Princesses!" Vamist said in the tones of someone grasping desperately for a straw. "It's traditional for dragons to eat princesses, not people."

Cimorene frowned. "Princesses are people. Some of them aren't very sensible, but they're still people."

"And anyway, dragons don't eat princesses," Kazul said. "We never have. I don't know how that silly story ever got started."

"I'm afraid you're mistaken, madam," Vamist said. "Rathenmor Quillen says quite clearly in his *Observations of Magical Beasts* that—"

"Rathenmor Quillen was an idiot," Kazul said. "And so, it seems, are you."

"Got it in one," said Scorn. "He's as dumb as that rabbit."

"I'm not dumb," said Killer. "I'm hungry. I just thought I'd mention it, in case you'd forgotten."

"Rathenmor Quillen, an idiot?" Vamist's outrage got the better of both his terror and his good sense, and he drew himself up stiffly and glared at Kazul. "How dare you say such a thing about the greatest scholar of the past two hundred years! Who do you think you are?"

"I say it because it's true." Kazul smiled, starting slowly and letting the corners of her mouth draw back farther and farther until all of her sharp, shiny silver teeth were exposed in a fierce grin. "And I'm the King of the Dragons."

"Ah, er—oh, ah—" said Vamist, deflating abruptly.

"Cimorene, when you're finished with this fellow, whoever he is, I believe I'd like to see how he tastes," Kazul went on. "Unless you want to save him for later, of course."

"I don't know," said Cimorene. "He's certainly caused a lot of trouble, but I'm not sure he deserves to be eaten."

"He hasn't got any manners," Kazul said. "That's enough for me. And I could do with some dessert."

"Could you stop talking about food?" Killer said plaintively.

"So if you haven't got any better ideas . . . " Kazul said.

Morwen smiled suddenly. "I think perhaps I have one that's more . . . appropriate. If you'll forgo your dessert, Kazul, I'd like to—"

"What dessert?" asked Trouble, strolling into the center of the group. "I thought all the wizards were gone. Oh, and does anyone want to know what I found in the castle, or are you busy with other things right now?"

21

In Which Nobody Is Satisfied

No one except Morwen and the other animals—Killer, Kazul, Scorn, and Horatio—understood what Trouble had asked, but everyone, even Vamist, could tell by their reactions that it was important.

"All right, hotshot, what did you find in the castle?" asked Scorn, switching her tail in annoyance at having to admit to so much curiosity in public.

"One moment, please," Morwen said. Quickly, she explained to Cimorene, Telemain, Brandel, and Amory where Trouble had been and what he had just said. Cimorene bit her lip, glanced at Vamist, and turned to Willin. "Willin, can you keep this fellow under control and out of the way? He was working with the wizards, and I don't think he should hear this."

"He may have some insight to offer, Your Majesty," said the elf. "However, if you wish it, I will do my best."

"I'll get his insights later," Cimorene said grimly. "Get him out of here."

"I'll help," Amory offered.

"Me, too," said Brandel. "I'd be quite happy to help, in fact."

Vamist looked at the two fire-witches, who were eyeing him the same way Murgatroyd and Chaos tended to eye a particularly plump mouse, and blanched.

"Thank you," Cimorene said to Brandel. "Just leave enough of him for me to get some answers out of later."

"I think we can manage that," said Brandel.

Willin bowed and the three of them marched Vamist off into the forest. Cimorene turned back to Trouble. "Morwen . . ."

Morwen nodded at the cat. "Go ahead now, but slowly, so I can translate."

"Couldn't you just let them wonder?" asked Trouble. "Oh, all right. The castle is empty, except for the usual furniture and a couple of gooey wizards' robes. I'd guess Mendanbar melted a few of them before they got him."

"Got him?" Cimorene said after Morwen's translation. "What does he mean by that, Morwen?"

"If she doesn't interrupt, I'll tell you." Trouble was plainly enjoying all the attention. "I didn't see any trace of Mendanbar, so I asked the gargoyle in the study—the one that answers the magic mirror—if it knew what happened. Apparently, the wizards didn't notice that it was intelligent, so they did quite a bit of talking in front of it."

"What did they say?" Killer asked with the air of someone interested in spite of himself.

"Oh, this and that. Most of it wasn't very interesting."

Kazul put one forearm down next to Trouble and flexed claws that were almost as long as the cat's tail. "Little one, tell your story without these digressions, or I may lose what little patience the Society of Wizards has left me."

"If you insist." Trouble stretched, to show that even a dragon couldn't impress *him*, then went on. "The gargoyle said I was right about the robes: Zemenar and his group lost four wizards before they managed to corner Mendanbar. The gargoyle knew about it because they all came into the study afterward to decide what to do next. Seems that the wizards found out that they couldn't kill a King of the Enchanted Forest outright without messing up what they were doing to the forest. And Zemenar didn't want to just hold him prisoner, because he was afraid we would come back any minute." Trouble shook his head in admiration. "You know, Mendanbar's almost as good as a cat."

"At what?" asked Morwen. "Oh, never mind. What did they do with him?"

"Zemenar put him in storage," said Trouble.

"What does *that* mean?" Cimorene asked once Morwen had translated this.

Trouble shrugged. "He sent Mendanbar somewhere where he couldn't make any difficulties while the wizards finished up with the forest. 'I'll put him through a door and then hide the door,' is what the gargoyle heard him say. Too bad Zemenar didn't work the spell in the study where old wooden-head could watch, or I might have been able to tell you what it means."

"This doesn't make any sense." Cimorene sounded thoroughly frustrated.

"Of course it doesn't make sense," Scorn said. "Wizards don't *have* sense. If they did, they wouldn't make all these problems."

Morwen did not translate Scorn's comment. Instead, she asked Trouble, "Where did the wizards do their spell? Could you tell?"

"Piece of cake," Trouble said. "In the Grand Hall. The place reeked of recent spell casting, and—"

"Did you check the rest of the castle?" Morwen interrupted. "The Grand Hall is where Telemain did his wizard-liquefication spell, and you may have been sensing the residue from that."

"Give me credit for some sense," Trouble said. "Besides, it's not that hard to tell Telemain's magic from a wizard's. Even though they used some of his equipment."

"I still don't understand," Killer complained. "And—"

"And you're hungry," said Scorn. "We know."

"I don't understand either," said Cimorene. "What does 'put him through a door and then hide the door' *mean?*"

"Telemain?" said Morwen.

"Mmmm. It sounds as if someone did a partial transportation spell, looped it, bound the residual to a temporary construct, and then—"

Kazul cleared her throat pointedly. Telemain paused, frowned, and said crossly, "I don't know any other way to explain it."

"They used a transportation spell to send Mendanbar somewhere, only they stopped in the middle," Morwen suggested.

"No, that would be unstable," Telemain said. "The field would collapse unless they looped it and bound the ends to something. It's theoretically possible, but it takes an enormous amount of power."

Cimorene glanced over her shoulder at the destruction that surrounded the castle. "As much power as you'd get from soaking up a big chunk of the Enchanted Forest?"

"I think they used most of that for the shield spell," Telemain said. "But if anyone could have done a looped transport, Zemenar could. After all, he was Head Wizard of the Society of Wizards."

"I don't care if he was First Minister to the Grand Poobah of the Great Cathayan Empire," Cimorene said. "How are we going to get Mendanbar *out?*"

"We can't," Telemain said.

"What?"

"To dismantle the spell, we would need to be inside the castle. To get into the castle, we would have to get through the wizards' shield spell. The only thing—besides the Society of Wizards themselves—that can take down that shield spell is Mendanbar's sword. And none of us can use it."

Cimorene looked appalled. "Then Mendanbar's stuck *forever.*"

"Or until he starves to death," Killer put in gloomily.

"Not necessarily," Morwen said. Everyone turned to look at her. "In the first place, if Telemain is right about what they did, Mendanbar won't starve. A looped transportation spell makes it temporarily unnecessary to eat."

Telemain nodded, pleased. "Hershenfeld's experiments proved it. They were quite definitive."

"In the second place, it is only true that none of us can use the sword *yet*." Morwen pushed her glasses firmly up and gave Cimorene a significant look.

"What—oh, Morwen, you can't mean the *baby!*" said Cimorene.

"Sounds reasonable to me," said Killer.

"It would," said Scorn.

Telemain frowned. "I don't think it will work, Morwen. The sword requires a certain level of deliberate control, and I doubt that a baby could provide coherent directions."

"We'll wait for him to grow," Kazul said. "It won't take long."

"Maybe not by dragon standards," Cimorene said. "But fifteen or sixteen years is a long time for people. I don't want to wait. And what if he's a she?"

"That shouldn't make any difference," Telemain said. "What's important to the sword is the bloodline and the—the personality. Or perhaps it's attitude that counts. I've never actually seen the linkage process that enables someone to use the sword, so I can't say for sure."

"No," said Cimorene. "Absolutely not. It would take too long, and it's too iffy. And what if one of the wizards decides to come back and sneak into the castle to finish Mendanbar off?"

"Have you got any better ideas?" Kazul asked.

"How about lunch?" Killer said pointedly. "Aren't people supposed to think better when they've eaten? I do."

"It wouldn't take much," Scorn said. "You're a rabbit."

"Not anymore." Killer's ears went limp and his wings drooped at the thought. "Now I'm a—a something else."

"Lunch sounds like a very good idea to me," Kazul said. "Especially since we needn't rush right in to rescue Mendanbar."

Looking suddenly uneasy, Killer backed away from the dragon. All at once, he stopped and his eyes got very big. "You *can't* eat me! I'm insubstantial." His muzzle twitched. "I never thought there'd be anything good about that."

"I'm not interested in eating you," Kazul said. "What I want is six gallons of Morwen's cider and a big helping of cherries jubilee."

Morwen frowned. "I thought you were full."

"I'm never too full for dessert," said the dragon. "And chasing wizards is thirsty work."

"I suppose we might as well," Cimorene said. "It doesn't look as if any of you will make much sense otherwise."

"Does that mean someone is going to fix me?" said Killer.

"I thought you wanted to stay insubstantial," Trouble said with a sly glance in Kazul's direction.

"Not if it means I can't eat."

Since this was an eminently reasonable attitude, and since Killer had been very patient, all things considered, Telemain agreed to take a look at the spells afflicting Killer. While Kazul called in various dragons and fire-witches to set up lunch, Telemain unloaded a large number of peculiar-looking implements from his pockets and began stalking around the donkey, muttering under his breath. Morwen, after a moment's consideration, chose to help Telemain rather than assist with lunch. It gave her a fighting chance of keeping the magician from getting so absorbed in studying the interconnecting layers of enchantment that he forgot about removing them.

They were, it turned out, just in time. The various enchantments seemed almost to have taken on a life of their own, linking and intertwining with each other until there was no separating them. Fortunately, Killer's insubstantiality had only just begun to be incorporated into the main mass, but even so it took the combined efforts of Morwen and Telemain to nullify it. The process was slow, and by the time they finished they stood in the center of a circle of interested observers attracted by the spectacle of a six-foot-something blue donkey with wings blinking on and off as bits of the spell came loose.

"Whew!" said Telemain when the last of the insubstantiality had been removed and canceled out. "That was more of a job than I expected."

"Can you stop now?" Cimorene asked. "Lunch is ready. If you could leave the rest of the spells for afterward—"

"I think we're going to have to leave the rest of the spells for good," Telemain said, stowing his implements back in their appropriate pockets.

"What?"

"Killer has so much magic stuck to him that the bottom layers have melted together," Morwen said. "It's practically impossible to undo the spells he's under. We were lucky to get the top layer off."

"You mean I'm going to be a seven-foot, eleven-inch—counting the ears—bright blue floating donkey with oversized wings for the rest of my *life?*" Killer wailed.

"Count your blessings," said Scorn. "At least you're not insubstantial anymore."

"And you're not a rabbit," Trouble pointed out. "That's a plus."

"But I'm *supposed* to be a rabbit!"

"Quiet," Morwen told them sternly. "As I was saying, *undoing* the spells is next to impossible. But *moving* them . . ."

". . . is elementary magic," Telemain said, nodding. "We won't even need any special equipment. But who were you thinking of moving them to?"

Morwen smiled. "Cimorene, would you ask Willin to bring Arona Michaelear Grinogion Vamist over here for a moment, please? This won't take long, and then we can relax and have lunch."

For a moment, Cimorene and Telemain stared at Morwen, and then they began to smile, too. "It will be my pleasure," Cimorene said, and called Willin over. A short time later, Vamist appeared, flanked by Brandel and Amory.

"What do you want now?" Vamist asked. "I *demand* that you send me home at once."

"In a minute," Morwen said. "Stand over here by Killer. Trouble, Scorn—"

"Right here," Scorn purred. "Go ahead whenever you're ready."

"Good." Morwen raised her left hand, palm up, then flipped it over.

"Front to back,
White to black,
Young to old,
Silver to gold."

As she finished speaking, Killer began to glow green. The glow pulsed once, brightly, far enough for the edge to touch Vamist. "Whoops!" said Vamist, and "Eek!" said Killer, and then an ordinary brown rabbit with a few faded patches of white-dyed fur dropped to the ground next to an oversized blue floating donkey with wings.

"Look," said Scorn. "He's got a little bald patch between his ears."

"What—eee-augh!" said Vamist. "No! You can't *do* this to me!"

"Want to bet?" said Trouble.

"Goodness, he looks silly," said Killer, twitching his nose. "Is that really what I was like?"

"Except for the bald patch," said Scorn.

"You can't mean to leave me like this!" Vamist cried. "You wouldn't make me stay a *donkey!*"

"You're not just *a* donkey," Morwen said, letting her smile grow. "You're a seven-foot bright blue floating donkey with oversized wings. And as far as I'm concerned you can stay that way for the rest of your life. Telemain, have you got enough energy left to send him to the main square in his hometown?"

"I believe I can manage that," Telemain said.

"No! I'll be the laughingstock of the whole countryside! And how will I get people to pay attention to what I say?"

"You won't," Brandel said with considerable relish. "No one will listen to someone who looks that silly. Morwen, it's perfect."

"It certainly is," Cimorene said. "How on earth did you think of it?"

"It came to me a while back, when Scorn said he was 'as dumb as that rabbit.' Now all that's left is the problem of what to do about the castle."

But though they discussed it over lunch, after lunch, and through the afternoon until dinner, no one could think of anything that might work. Telemain spent an hour studying the shield spell, but he could not find any way to get rid of it. The dragons could not get close to it because the spell was too similar to the one on the wizards' staffs and made them sneeze. The fire-witches' magic just bounced off. In desperation, Cimorene even tried to stick Mendanbar's sword into the spell, but it stopped at the edge of the glow and refused to penetrate it.

"I think we're going to have to wait for the baby," Telemain said finally.

"I'm not giving up yet," Cimorene said. "There's *got* to be some way to get in, or to get Mendanbar out."

"Don't be so sure," Morwen said. "Barrier spells frequently come with a time delay, rather than any specific sort of key. I believe a hundred years is the usual period, though that normally applies to hedges of briars, not glowing magic shields. Still . . ."

"I'm not giving up," Cimorene repeated. "And I'm certainly not waiting a hundred years!"

And she didn't. For the next two months, while Telemain and Morwen disposed of Vamist the donkey and sent Killer the rabbit back to his clover patch, while the dragons combed the Enchanted Forest for stray wizards, while the fire-witches finished helping out and went home (or, in some cases, built new homes in the Enchanted Forest), Cimorene tried everything anyone could think of to get herself through the wizards' shield. She had dwarves dig tunnels and birds dive at the top of the shield; she sprayed it with soapy lemon water and sprinkled it with powdered dragon scales (donated for the purpose by Kazul); she cast spells alone at midnight and at noon in combination with Morwen, Telemain, all of the fire-witches, and several dragons.

Nothing made any difference.

Kazul left a squad of dragons to keep watch for wizards near the castle, and she herself visited frequently. Eventually, she persuaded Cimorene to slow down, at least until the baby was born. Since none of the other attempts had shown any sign of success, Cimorene's child seemed more and more to be their best hope of getting into the castle, rescuing Mendanbar, and defeating the wizards once and for all. Rumors began circulating, each purporting to give the real truth about the battle and the whereabouts of King Mendanbar.

The Society of Wizards was too busy with its own

affairs—choosing a new Head Wizard and recovering from the unexpected onslaught of dragons and fire-witches—to make new trouble for the time being. So the pause in the fighting stretched out longer and longer until it became a sort of uneasy, unofficial peace.

And everyone waited.

EPILOGUE

Which Hints at Things to Come

Motherhood suits Cimorene, Morwen thought as she watched the Queen of the Enchanted Forest and the King of the Dragons making peculiar noises over the infant Prince Daystar, aged two months, six days, and some-odd hours. On the moss beside them, at the foot of an ancient and enormous willow, lay Mendanbar's unsheathed sword.

"Telemain says he melted another wizard in the eastern part of the forest yesterday," Morwen said aloud. "They're getting bolder."

Cimorene looked up, her face clouded. "I know. Antorell found me this morning. It's all right. I melted him," she added quickly. "But he was very angry. I think he blames me because Kazul ate his father."

"Antorell never was very strong on logic," Kazul said. "Ooochy-ooo. *What* a fine big boy you are!"

Since this last was directed at the baby Prince,

Morwen only smiled. "It's a good thing none of my cats are here, or you'd have to make an equal fuss the next time one of them has kittens."

"As long as I don't have to be their godmother, I'll be happy to fuss," Kazul said.

"I didn't know your cats were expecting kittens," Cimorene said.

"None of them is, yet." Morwen smiled again. "Though the way Scorn and Horatio are behaving, it's only a matter of time. You should hear some of the things Trouble says about them—'mushy' is probably the kindest."

"It's a good thing you like cats," Cimorene said.

"Yes, it is." Morwen looked at Cimorene, and her smile faded. "You're avoiding the real subject, which is, *What are you going to do now?* It will be a long time before Daystar is old enough to use Mendanbar's sword, and if the Society of Wizards is looking for him—"

"I don't think they are," Cimorene said. "I don't think they even know Daystar exists. Mendanbar and I hadn't officially announced it before they attacked, and afterward it seemed like a good idea to keep quiet about it. So they haven't heard, and they're not looking for Daystar. They're looking for the sword, and they're looking for me."

"It amounts to the same thing," Morwen said. "And doesn't Antorell know about Daystar, if he found you this morning?"

Cimorene snorted. "Antorell was so mad at me that he didn't notice anything else. He walked right by the sword and tripped over Kazul's tail before I melted him."

"Still, if he found you, it's only a matter of time before the rest of the Society does, too. Isn't it?"

"Not quite." Cimorene glanced sideways at Kazul and took a deep breath. "I've thought about this a lot, and I have an idea how to outsmart them. I want to know what you think of it."

"You know what *I* think of it," Kazul rumbled. "I don't like it one bit. The idea of—"

"Hush, Kazul, you'll upset Daystar. It's like this, Morwen: The Society of Wizards knows I've brought Mendanbar's sword back to the Enchanted Forest, because they can't swallow big chunks of the forest's magic anymore and they know that the sword is what keeps them from doing that. So they're poking around here, looking for me and the sword. If I leave the forest—"

"But you can't take the sword out of the Enchanted Forest or the Society of Wizards will start destroying it again," Morwen said. "Or else the sword will leak all the magic out of the forest, which amounts to the same thing."

"I'm not going to take the sword out of the Enchanted Forest," Cimorene said. "I'm going to hide it in here, and then I'm going to take Daystar and settle down outside the forest somewhere. Not with the dragons; the wizards will expect that."

Morwen frowned, forcing herself to consider the proposal carefully. "So the Society of Wizards will look for you inside the Enchanted Forest, because they'll expect you to be with the sword and they'll know that the sword is still inside the forest. And since you'll be *outside* the forest, you and Daystar will be relatively safe. And things won't get any worse *inside* the forest, because the sword will keep the wizards from destroying new bits. Very neat. But what if they find the sword?"

"I don't think they will," Cimorene said. "Telemain did some experiments with a wizard's staff, and he says that as long as the sword is inside the Enchanted Forest, it's invisible to wizards' magic. If I hide it well, they'll have to search the whole forest, inch by inch, on foot, in order to find it."

"And I doubt any of them have the patience for that. But are you sure that the wizards won't think up a way to get around it?"

"Telemain says that the only way a wizard could use magic to find the sword would be to use a spell that finds the person who's carrying it. And for *that* to work, the person carrying it has to know that what he's got is Mendanbar's sword. That's why I can't give it to you or Telemain."

"I see. So by the time the wizards think of casting that type of spell, if they ever do, the sword will be hidden and you'll be outside the forest."

Cimorene nodded. "I'd like to have you or Telemain check on the sword once in a while to make sure it's all right, but if the wizards start looking for someone who knows what it is—"

"That shouldn't be a problem as long as we don't try to carry it." Morwen's right hand tingled, remembering the way it had burned when she held it. "And I certainly don't intend to try!"

"Oh, that only happens outside the Enchanted Forest," Cimorene said, then frowned. "At least, I'm fairly sure that's what Telemain meant when he explained. Inside the Enchanted Forest, the sword does different things."

"Well, I'm not giving it the chance to do them to me," Morwen said. "If you want to be certain the wizards won't catch us checking, I'll send one of the cats."

"That should work. Not too often."

"No, we wouldn't want to lead the Society of Wizards right to it." Morwen shook her head. "I don't like it any more than Kazul does, but it sounds as if it will work. As far as it goes."

"As far as it goes? What do you think I've forgotten?"

"The Society of Wizards put up that shield spell. What if they decide to pull it down in a year or two and take over the castle? We can't keep a guard on it for the next sixteen or twenty years. Not an effective one, anyway."

"Speak for yourself," Kazul said. "Sixteen or twenty years of guarding a castle is nothing to a dragon."

"And Kazul and Telemain have already solved that problem anyway," Cimorene said. "You must not have come by the castle, or you'd have seen it."

"Seen what?" said Morwen.

"The second shield spell, the one the dragons put up." Cimorene's eyes sparked. "Telemain analyzed the wizards' shield spell, and then Kazul got all the dragons to duplicate it. It works the same way the Society's spell does: only the people who put it up can take it down."

Morwen pursed her lips. "So we can't get at the castle because of the wizards' spell, and the wizards can't get at their spell because of the dragons' spell. You do seem to have thought of everything."

"Thank you," said Kazul. "Now convince Cimorene that she'll be safe in the Mountains of Morning with the rest of us, and we'll be all set."

"I don't think I can do that," Morwen said. "In the first place, Cimorene is stubborn as a pig when she wants to be, and in the second place, she's right. As soon as the Society of Wizards figures out she's not in the Enchanted Forest, they'll look for her with dragons. And they're sneaky enough to find her, and that would ruin everything." She sighed. "When do you intend to leave, Cimorene?"

"This afternoon, as soon as I hide this." Cimorene picked up the sword. "It's a pity I can't put it in a sheath, but Telemain says that with Mendanbar . . . unavailable, a sheath would obstruct some of the sword's spells that interfere with wizards."

"Would you like some help?" Morwen said.

"It can't hurt. Kazul, will you watch Daystar for an hour or two?"

"I suppose so. Since you seem determined."

"Good." Cimorene patted the dragon's shoulder. "And thank you. Bye, Daystar."

As she bent forward to kiss him, the flash of light on the blade of the sword caught the child's attention, and he reached for it with both hands. "Ah-ah-ah!" he demanded.

"No, Daystar," Cimorene replied gently. "Not now. This is for later, when you're older."

"Ah-ah-*ah!*" said Daystar emphatically.

"When you're older," Cimorene said again. "Come on, Morwen, let's get started." Together they walked through the trees to find a place to hide the sword against the time when Daystar would be old enough to use it.

Cimorene's adventures continue in . . .

Talking to Dragons

The fourth book in the Enchanted Forest Chronicles

Turn the page for an exciting sneak peak!

1

In Which Daystar Leaves Home and Encounters a Lizard

Mother taught me to be polite to dragons. Particularly polite, I mean; she taught me to be ordinary polite to everyone. Well, it makes sense. With all the enchanted princesses and disguised wizards and transformed kings and so on wandering around, you never know *whom* you might be talking to. But dragons are a special case.

Not that I ever actually talked to one until after I left home. Even at the edge of the Enchanted Forest, dragons aren't exactly common. The principle is what matters, though: *Always* be polite to a dragon. It's harder than it sounds. Dragon etiquette is incredibly complicated, and if you make a mistake, the dragon eats you. Fortunately, I was well trained.

Dragon etiquette wasn't the only thing Mother taught me. Reading and writing are unusual skills for a poor boy, but I learned them. Music, too, and fighting. Don't ask me where Mother learned to use a sword. Until I was thirteen, I didn't know we had one in the house. I even learned a little magic. Mother wasn't exactly pleased; but growing up on the edge of the Enchanted Forest, I had to know some things.

Mother is tall—about two inches taller than I am —and slender, and very impressive when she wants to be. Her hair is black, like mine, but much longer. Most of the time she wears it in two braids wound around and around her head, but when she really wants to impress someone she lets it hang straight to her feet. A lot of the disguised princes who stopped at our cottage on their way into the Enchanted Forest thought Mother was a sorceress. You can't really blame them. Who else would live at the edge of a place like that?

Sometimes I thought they were right. Mother always knew what directions to give them, even if they didn't tell her what they were looking for. I never saw her do any real magic, though, until the day the wizard came.

I knew right away that he was a wizard. Not because of his brown beard or his blue-and-brown silk robes—although no one but a wizard can walk around in blue-and-brown silk robes for very long without getting really dusty. It wasn't even his staff. I knew he was a wizard because he had the same *feel* of magic that the unicorns and griffins have when you catch a glimpse of them, farther on in the forest.

I was surprised to see him because we didn't get too many wizards. Well, actually, we'd never gotten any. Mother said that most of them preferred to go into the forest through the Gates of Mist and Pearl at the top of the Crystal Falls, or through the Caves of Fire and Night if they could manage it. The few that went into the forest in other ways never stopped at our cottage.

This wizard was unusual. He turned off the road and walked right past me without saying anything, straight up to our cottage. Then he banged on the door with the head of his staff. The door splintered and fell apart.

I decided that I didn't like him.

Mother was cooking rabbit stew in the big black pot over the chimney fire. She didn't even look up when the door fell in. The wizard stood there for a minute, and I sneaked a little closer so I could see better. He was frowning, and I got the impression he wasn't used to being ignored. Mother kept stirring the stew.

"Well, Cimorene, I have found you," the wizard said at last.

"It took you long enough," Mother said without turning. "You're getting slow."

"You know why I am here."

Mother shrugged. "You're sixteen years too late. I told you, you're getting slow."

"Ha! I can take the sword now, and the boy as well. There is nothing you can do to stop me this time," the wizard said. I could tell he was trying to sound menacing, but he didn't do a very good job.

Mother finally turned around. I took one look at her face and backed up a couple of steps. She looked at the wizard for a minute and started to smile. "Nothing, Antorell? Are you sure?"

The wizard laughed and raised his staff. I backed up some more. I mean, I wanted to see what was going on, but I'm not *stupid*. He paused a moment—for effect, I think—and Mother pointed at him.

"Argelfraster," she said, and he started to melt.

"No! Not *again*!" he screamed. He shrank pretty quickly—all but his head, which was shouting nearly the whole time. "I'll get you, Cimorene! I'll be back! You can't stop me! I'll—"

Then his head collapsed and there was nothing left but a little puddle of brown goo and his staff.

I stared at the puddle. All I could think was, *I never knew Mother could do that*. Mother let me stand there for a while before she told me to clean it up.

"Don't touch the staff," she said. "And don't forget to wash your hands before you come to dinner."

I went to get a bucket. When I came back, the staff was gone and Mother was stirring the stew as if nothing had happened. She didn't mention the wizard again until the next morning.

I was out by the remains of our door, trying to fix it. I didn't think my chances were very good. I picked up the hammer, and as I looked around for nails I saw Mother walk out of the Enchanted Forest. I was so surprised I dropped the hammer and nearly smashed my foot. Mother never went into the Enchanted Forest. Never. Then I saw the sword she was carrying, and if I'd still been holding the hammer, I'd have dropped it again.

Even from a distance, I could tell it wasn't an ordinary sword. It was about the same size and shape as the one I practiced with, but it shone too brightly and looked too sharp to be ordinary. Mother brought it over to me and set it down on top of the boards I'd been working on. "Don't touch it," she said, and went into the house.

I had a hard time following Mother's instructions. The more I looked at the sword, the more I wanted to pick it up and try a few of the passes Mother had taught me. It was such a beautiful weapon! Just looking at it made me shiver. But Mother always had good reasons for the things she told me to do, so I waited.

I didn't have to wait long. She came back almost immediately, carrying a sword belt and a sheath that I'd never seen before. They were old—so old that the leather had turned nearly gray—and very, very plain. I was disappointed; the sword deserved something more impressive.

Mother went straight to the sword and put it in the sheath. She relaxed a little then, as if she'd been worried about something. Mother almost never worried. I started wondering just what that weapon did. I didn't have much time to think about it, though. As soon as she had sheathed the sword, Mother turned and gave me her You're-not-much-but-you'll-have-to-do look. *I* started to worry.

Mother picked up the sword belt. "This is for you, Daystar." I reached for it, but she shook her head. "No, I'll do it this first time. Hold still."

She bent down and buckled the belt around my waist, then hung the sheathed sword on the belt. I felt a little strange letting her do all that, and my elbows kept getting in the way.

Finally she straightened up. "Now, Daystar, I have a few things to tell you before you leave."

"Leave?" I was shocked. Mother had never mentioned leaving before. It occurred to me that she'd said "you," not "we." I swallowed hard. "By myself?"

"Of course. You're sixteen; it's time you left, and I'm certainly not coming with you. Now pay attention." She gave me one of her sharp looks.

I paid attention.

"You have a sword, and you know as much as I can safely teach you. I don't want to see you back here again until you can explain to me why you had to leave. Do you understand?"

I nodded.

Mother went on, "Start with the Enchanted Forest. One way or another, things will happen more quickly there. Don't lose your sword, and don't draw it unless you need to use it. Oh, and watch out for Antorell. It'll take him a couple of days to get himself back together and find out where I put his staff, but once he does he'll try to make trouble again. All right?"

"But you haven't explained anything!" I blurted. "Why did that wizard come here yesterday, anyway? Why should he want to make trouble for me? And if he's so dangerous, why are you sending me—"

"Daystar!"

I stopped in midsentence.

Mother glared at me. "What happened to the manners I've tried to teach you?"

"I—I'm sorry, Mother," I said. "I was upset."

"Being upset is no excuse," Mother said sternly. "If you're going to be rude, do it for a reason and get something from it."

I nodded.

Mother smiled. "I know it's hard, and it's rather short notice, but this will probably be the best chance we get. I can't waste it just to give you time to get used to the idea of leaving home. Besides, if I tell you too much now, it could ruin everything. You'll just have to work things out for yourself."

I was more confused than ever, but I could see Mother wasn't going to tell me anything else. She looked at me for another moment, then bit her lip as if she wanted to say something and couldn't. Abruptly, she turned and walked away. At the door of the cottage, she stopped and looked back. "Good luck, Daystar. And stop wasting time. You don't have much of it." Before I could say anything, she disappeared inside.

I started off toward the Enchanted Forest. Mother's advice was always good. Besides, I was afraid she'd melt me or something if I hung around very long.

I didn't bother to follow the road. It isn't particularly useful, anyway—it disappears as soon as you cross into the forest. Or at least, it usually does. At any rate, I wanted to start with the section of the Enchanted Forest that I knew.

The Enchanted Forest comes in two parts, the Outer Forest and the Deep Woods. Most people don't realize that. The Outer Forest is relatively safe if you know what you're doing, and I'd gathered herbs there a few times. I'd never gone more than an hour's walk from our cottage, and nothing particularly interesting had ever happened, but I'd always known that something might. The way things were going, I was pretty sure that this time something would.

I felt the little tingle on my skin that marks the border between the ordinary woods, where our cottage was, and the Enchanted Forest. Some people have trouble getting in and out of the Enchanted Forest, but I never did. I was feeling excited and adventurous, and maybe a little scared. I mean, for years I'd watched all those princes and heroes and so on go into the forest, and now it was my turn. I looked back over my shoulder to see if Mother was watching. The cottage was gone.

That shook me. You just don't expect the place you've lived in for sixteen years to vanish like that. I looked around. The trees were huge—much larger than the ones by our cottage. I couldn't reach more than a quarter of the way around the trunk of the smallest one. The ground was covered with dark green moss that ran right up to the bases of the trees and stopped short. I could see a couple of bushes, including one that had three different colors of flowers on it. Everything felt very dark and green and alive, and none of it looked familiar at all.

I shivered. This wasn't the Outer Forest. This was the Deep Woods.

I waited for a couple of minutes, but nothing happened. Somehow, I wasn't reassured. Being lost in the Enchanted Forest does not do much for one's peace of mind.

After a while I started walking again. I felt much less adventurous and considerably more scared.

I walked for a long time. Eventually I quit being scared, at least mostly. Finally I started looking for a place to rest; my feet hurt and I was getting very tired. I was careful, though. I didn't want to sit on a flower that used to be someone important. After about fifteen minutes I found a spot that looked all right, and I started to sit down. Unfortunately, I'd forgotten I was wearing the sword. It got tangled up in my legs and I sort of fell over.

Somebody giggled. I looked around and didn't see anyone, so I decided to get untangled first. I straightened my legs out and sat up, making sure the sword belt was out of the way this time. Then I took a second look around. I still didn't see anyone, but the same somebody giggled again.

"Sir or madam or—" I stopped. What was the proper honorific for something that wasn't male or female? I was pretty sure there was one, but I couldn't remember it.

"Oh, don't bother," said a high, squeaky voice. "I've never cared for all that fancy stuff."

I still didn't see anyone. "Forgive my stupidity, but I can't seem to find where you are," I said.

The giggle came again. "Down here, silly."

I looked down and jumped. A little gold lizard was sitting right next to my hand. He was about twice as long as my middle finger, and half of that was tail.

"Hey, watch it!" said the lizard. "You might hurt someone if you keep jumping around like that. Me, for instance. You big people are so careless."

"I'm very sorry," I said politely.

The lizard lifted his head. "You are? Yes, you are! How amazing. Who are you, anyway?"

"My name is Daystar," I said, bowing slightly. It was a little awkward to do from a sitting position, but I managed. Being polite to a lizard felt peculiar, but there are only two rules of behavior in the Enchanted Forest: Don't take anything for granted, and Be polite to everyone. That's if you don't live there. The inhabitants have their own codes, which it's better not to ask about.

"You're Daystar?" The lizard did something very tangled very quickly and ended up balanced on his tail. "So you are! Well, my goodness. I hadn't expected to see you around here for a while yet."

"You were expecting me?"

"Of course." The lizard looked smug. "I know everything that goes on in the Enchanted Forest. Absolutely *everything*! I've seen you in the Outer Forest. It was only a matter of time before you got this far, though I thought it would take longer. I'm Suz, by the way."

"Pleased to meet you," I said.

"You are?" The lizard leaned forward and almost lost his balance. "Yes, you really are! How positively extraordinary. Whatever are you doing in the Enchanted Forest?"

"I don't know," I said.

"You don't know!" The lizard did a back flip and

scurried up onto a fat tree root, where he would have a better view. He balanced on his tail again and looked at me thoughtfully. "If you don't know what you're doing, why are you here?"

I thought for a moment. "Do you really know everything that happens in this forest?"

"Of course I do." Suz looked offended. An offended lizard is an interesting sight.

"I didn't mean to hurt your feelings or anything," I said hastily. "I just wondered if you could tell me where this came from." I touched the sword Mother had given me.

The lizard squinted in my general direction. "What? It's on the wrong side of you, silly. Bring it over where I can see it. If it came from the Enchanted Forest, I can tell you about it."

I lifted the sword, sheath and all, and twisted it around so it was on the same side of me as Suz. The lizard promptly fell over backward.

"Oh dear me my gracious goodness my oh," he squeaked. "Do you know what that *is*?"

"I wouldn't have asked you if I knew," I said. "It's a sword. I think it's magic."

"It's a sword! He thinks it's magic!" Suz ran around twice in a small circle, then did the tail-balancing trick again. "Where did you get it?" the little lizard demanded.

"My mother gave it to me. She got it out of the Enchanted Forest somewhere." I was getting a little tired of this. "Are you going to answer my question?"

"Your mother gave it to you. The Sword of the Sleeping King, that everyone in the world has been looking for for fifteen or twenty years, and *your mother gave it to you*." The lizard got so agitated he fell over again. "That isn't right. That isn't reasonable. My dear boy, that simply isn't done! Even in the Enchanted Forest there is a proper order for these things! Someone will have to notify them at the castle immediately. Oh, dear, what a stir this will cause!"

"I'm sorry, I didn't know. What's the Sword of the Sleeping King?" I'd never heard of it before, which rather surprised me. After Mother made me memorize all those pages of names and titles and peculiar weapons, I'd thought I knew the name of every magic sword in the world.

"You don't know?" The lizard froze in the middle of getting back up on his tail. He looked like a golden pretzel. "No, you don't! Oh, my. You'd better go to the castle at once. Kazul will know what to do with you. I'd better go there myself, right away." Suz untwisted and darted off into the undergrowth.

"Wait!" I shouted. "What castle? Who is Kazul? And why—"

The lizard looked back. "I don't have time for that! And even if I did, I couldn't tell you. You have to find out yourself. Magic swords always work that way. Don't you know *anything*?"

"Do you want me to recite the names of the Four Hundred Minor Swords of Korred the Spellsmith? . . . I know lots of things. I just don't know about this. How do I find out?"

"Follow the sword, silly," Suz said, and disappeared among the leaves.